The ABC Murders

Agatha Christie

Level 4

Retold by Anne Collins

Series Editors: Andy Hopkins and Jocelyn Potter

Pearson Education Limited
Edinburgh Gate, Harlow,
Essex CM20 2JE, England
and Associated Companies throughout the world.

ISBN: 978-1-4082-3205-7

This edition first published by Pearson Education Ltd 2010

7 9 10 8 6

Illustrations by Steve James

Set in 11/13pt A. Garamond
Printed in China
SWTC/06

Penguin Books Ltd a Penguin Random House company

Acknowledgements
We are grateful to the following for permission to reproduce photographs:
(Key: b-bottom; c-centre; l-left; r-right; t-top)
Corbis: Eye Ubiquitous / Paul Thompson 90

All other images © Pearson Education

Picture research by Frances Topp

Every effort has been made to trace the copyright holders and we apologise in advance for
any unintentional omissions. We would be pleased to insert the appropriate acknowledgement
in any subsequent edition of this publication.

For a complete list of the titles available in the Penguin Active Reading series please
write to your local Pearson Longman office or to: Penguin Readers Marketing Department,
Pearson Education, Edinburgh Gate, Harlow, Essex CM20 2JE, England.

Contents

1.1 What's the book about?

Answer the questions.

1 Agatha Christie is world-famous for her crime stories. List people, things and
events that you expect to read about in a crime story. Then compare your list
with the lists of other students. Do you agree?

.... police officers ....

....

....

2 Have you read any other books by Agatha Christie, or seen any films or plays
of her stories? If you have, explain what the crime was and why it was difficult
for the detective to solve the case – but don't tell other students how the case
was solved! If you haven't, find information about Agatha Christie's work on the
Internet. Which titles do you recognise?

3 Why do you think this story is called *The ABC Murders*?

1.2 What happens first?

1 **Describe the two men in the picture.
What do you think the relationship
between them is?**

  a old friends

  b old enemies

  c teacher and student

  d brothers

2 **What year do you think it is?**

  a 2005

  b 1970

  c 1935

  d 1900

3 **Now read the title of Chapter 1 and the words in italics below it.
How do you think the men in the picture above feel about the letter?**

  a pleased   **b** uninterested   **c** worried   **d** angry

The Letter

Mr Hercule Poirot, You think you are very clever at solving
mysteries that are too difficult for our poor, stupid British police.

My name is Captain Arthur Hastings. My wife and I have a large farm in South America, but before I was married I lived in London. There I helped my friend, the famous Belgian detective Hercule Poirot, solve many crimes.

Poirot used to work with the police in Belgium, but he **retired** several years ago. Since retiring, though, he has become a very successful private detective. When the British police have a difficult crime which they cannot solve, they often ask Poirot to help them.

In June 1935 I came back to Britain for six months on business while my wife stayed in South America to manage the farm. I didn't know that, during that time, I was going to work with my old friend Poirot again.

Most of this story is my own personal experience. Sometimes, though, I have included information about events when I was not present myself. But I believe I have described the thoughts and feelings of the other people in the story correctly. Poirot has seen my work, and agrees that I have.

In my opinion, Poirot used his skills in a most clever and unusual way to solve a number of crimes which were different from any others that he had worked on. I shall call these crimes the ABC Murders.

◆

After arriving in England, I went almost immediately to visit Poirot. He had moved to a new flat in London and was very pleased to see me.

'You're looking wonderful, Poirot,' I said. 'You haven't aged at all. In fact, if it were possible, I would say that you have fewer grey hairs than the last time I saw you.'

Poirot smiled. 'And why is that not possible? It is quite true.'

'Do you mean your hair is turning from grey to black instead of from black to grey?' I said in surprise. 'That's very strange. It seems against nature.'

'As usual, Hastings,' said Poirot, 'you have a beautiful and un**suspicious** mind. You have not changed over the years. You notice a strange fact and explain it in the same breath without noticing that you are doing so!'

Poirot walked into his bedroom and returned with a bottle in his hand. I looked at it, then I understood. It was a bottle of black hair colouring.

'Poirot!' I cried. 'You've coloured your hair!'

---

retire /rɪˈtaɪə/ (v) to stop working, usually because you are too old to work
suspicious /səˈspɪʃəs/ (adj) thinking that something is wrong. If you *suspect* someone (a **suspect**), you think they may be guilty of a crime.

'Ah, you begin to understand!' said Poirot.

'I suppose next time I come home, I shall find you wearing a false moustache – or are you wearing one now?'

Poirot looked shocked. He has a large black moustache which he is very proud of.

'No, no, *mon ami**. A false moustache! How horrible!' He pulled his moustache to prove to me that it was real. 'I have never seen a moustache like mine in the whole of London.'

That was a very good thing, I thought privately. But I didn't want to hurt Poirot's feelings, so instead I changed the subject.

'Are you still working?' I asked. 'I know you actually retired years ago.'

'Yes, it is true,' replied Poirot. 'I tried to grow vegetables instead. But immediately, a murder happened – and I had to forget about the vegetables. And since then, whenever I say that a **case** will be my last, it is not. Each time I say: this is the end. But then something else happens. But I must say, my friend, that I do not like retirement at all. If I do not use my brain, it will stop working.'

'I see,' I said. 'So you still use your brain sometimes.'

'Exactly. But I choose my cases very carefully. You know, Hastings, in many ways I think you bring me luck.'

'Really?' I said. 'In what ways?'

'As soon as I heard you were coming, I said to myself: something will happen. Hastings and I will hunt criminals again together, just like the old days. But if so, it must not be ordinary business. It must be something' – he waved his hands excitedly – 'something very fine and special.'

'Well,' I said at last, smiling, 'has this excellent crime happened yet?'

'*Pas encore†*. At least – ' Poirot paused, and a look of worry came over his face. His voice sounded so strange that I looked at him in surprise.

Suddenly he crossed the room to a desk near the window. There were papers arranged carefully inside. He took one out, then passed it to me.

'Tell me, *mon ami*,' he said. 'What do you think of this?'

I took it from him with interest. It was a letter which had been typed on thick white notepaper:

Mr Hercule Poirot, You think you are very clever at solving mysteries that are too difficult for our poor, stupid British police. Let us see, Mr Clever Poirot, just how clever you can be. Perhaps you'll find this problem too difficult. Watch out for Andover, on the 21st of the month.

Yours, A B C

---

* *mon ami*: French for 'my friend'

† *pas encore*: French for 'not yet'

case /keɪs/ (n) an event, or events, that the police or detectives are trying to learn more about

I looked at the envelope. The address was typed, too.

'The postmark is London WC1,' said Poirot. 'Well, what is your opinion?'

I handed the letter back to him.

'It's from a madman, I suppose,' I said.

'That is all you can say?'

'Well – doesn't it sound like a madman to you?'

'Yes, my friend, it does.'

His voice was serious. I looked at him in surprise.

'You're worried, Poirot.'

'A madman, *mon ami*, is a serious matter. A madman is a very dangerous thing.'

'Yes, of course, that's true ... I hadn't thought about that. But it sounds more like a rather stupid kind of joke. Perhaps the sender was drunk.'

'You may be right, Hastings ...'

'What have you done about it?' I asked.

'What can one do? I showed the letter to our good friend, Chief **Inspector** Japp. He thought the same as you – that it was a stupid joke. They get letters like these every day at Scotland Yard*. I, too, have received them before, but there is something about *that* letter, Hastings, that I do not like ...'

Poirot shook his head. Then he picked up the letter and put it in the desk.

'If you really think it's serious, can't you do something?' I asked.

'As always, you are a man who wants action! But what *can* we do? The police have seen the letter but they, too, will do nothing. There are no fingerprints on it. There are no **clues** to the possible writer.'

'In fact, there is only your own feeling?'

'Not feeling, Hastings. Feeling is a bad word. It is my *knowledge* – my *experience* – that tells me something about that letter is wrong.'

He waved his hands about, then shook his head again.

'Well,' I said, 'the 21st is Friday. If a big robbery happens near Andover then – '

'Ah, what a *good* thing that would be!'

'A good thing?' I stared in surprise. The word seemed to be a very strange one to use. 'A robbery may be exciting, but surely it can't be a good thing!'

Poirot shook his head. 'You don't understand, my friend. It would be a good thing because it would clear my mind of the fear of something else.'

'Of what?'

'Murder,' said Hercule Poirot.

Mr Alexander Bonaparte Cust got up from his chair and looked near-sightedly round his bedroom. The furniture was old and the bedroom was not very clean. His back hurt from sitting in the same position for too long. As he stretched himself to his full height, you could see that he was quite a tall man, but he did not look tall because he **stooped**.

He went to a coat that was hanging on the back of the door, and took from the pocket a packet of cheap cigarettes and some matches. He lit a cigarette and then returned to the table. He picked up a railway guide and searched for some information inside it. Then he looked at a typewritten list of names. With a pen, he made a mark against one of the first names on the list.

It was Thursday, 20 June.

* Scotland Yard: the main building for London's police
Inspector /ɪnˈspektə/ (n) a British police officer with quite a high position
clue /kluː/ (n) something, like a piece of information, that helps to solve a crime or mystery
stoop /stuːp/ (v) to bend the top half of your body forwards and down

I had forgotten about the **anonymous** letter which Poirot had received, and the importance of the 21st. On the 22nd, Poirot received a visit from Chief Inspector Japp of Scotland Yard. We had known the Inspector for many years, and he welcomed me warmly.

'What a surprise!' he cried. 'It's just like the old days, seeing you with Monsieur* Poirot again. You're looking well, too. Your hair is just getting a little thin. Well, that's what happens to all of us.'

I always brushed my hair carefully across the top of my head, so I wasn't very pleased that Inspector Japp had noticed my thinning hair. But I decided not to get upset.

* Monsieur: the French word for 'Mr'
anonymous /əˈnɒnɪməs/ (adj) written by someone who does not want their name to be known

'Yes, we're all getting older,' I agreed.

'Except for Monsieur Poirot,' said Japp, smiling at my friend. 'His hair and moustache look wonderful. And since he retired, he's become very famous. Train mysteries, air mysteries, high society deaths – oh, he's here, there and everywhere. Have you heard about his anonymous letter?'

'I showed it to Hastings the other day,' said Poirot.

'Of course,' I said. 'I'd completely forgotten about it. What was the date in the letter?'

'Yesterday,' said Japp. 'That's why I've come here. I rang the police in Andover to see if anything had happened. But the letter is certainly a joke. A shop window was broken by children throwing stones, and a few people got drunk, but that's all.'

'I am very glad about that,' said Poirot.

'We get lots of letters like that every day,' said Japp, 'from people who have nothing better to do. They don't mean any harm. They're just looking for a bit of excitement.'

'I have been foolish to think that the matter was so serious,' Poirot agreed.

'Well, I must go,' said Japp, laughing. 'I just wanted to stop you worrying.'

After the Inspector had left, Poirot said, 'He does not change much, the good Japp, eh?'

'He looks much older,' I said. 'And his hair is going grey,' I added nastily.

'You know, Hastings, I have a very clever hairdresser,' said Poirot. 'He could put some false hair onto your head and brush your own hair over it –'

'Poirot!' I shouted. 'I'm not interested in your hairdresser. What's the matter with the top of my head?'

'Nothing – nothing at all,' said Poirot quickly.

'Well,' I said, feeling a little calmer. 'I'm sorry that that anonymous letter didn't lead to an interesting crime.'

'Yes, I was wrong about that,' said Poirot. 'I am too suspicious.'

The telephone rang and Poirot got up to answer it.

''Allo,' he said. 'Yes, it is Hercule Poirot speaking.'

He listened for a minute or two and then I saw his face change.

'*Mais oui** ... Yes, we will come ... Naturally ... It may be as you say ... Yes, I will bring it. *A tout à l'heure*† then.'

He put down the phone and came across the room to me.

'That was Japp speaking, Hastings. He had just got back to Scotland Yard. There was a message from Andover ...'

'Andover?' I cried excitedly.

---

* *mais oui:* French for 'yes, of course'
† *a tout à l'heure:* French for 'see you soon'

Poirot said slowly, 'An old woman has been found murdered. She had a little tobacco and newspaper shop. Her name is Ascher.'

I think I felt a little **disappointed**. I had expected something very unusual. The murder of a shopkeeper didn't sound very interesting.

Poirot continued in the same serious voice, 'The Andover police believe they know who did it. It seems that the woman's husband gets drunk and behaves badly. He has said several times that he would kill her.

'But the police would like to have another look at the anonymous letter I received. So I have said that you and I will go down to Andover at once.'

I felt a little more excited. Perhaps the murder of the old woman wasn't very interesting, but it was still a *crime*. It had been a long time since I had mixed with crime and criminals.

I wasn't really listening to Poirot's next words. But later I remembered them very clearly.

'This is the beginning,' said Hercule Poirot.

disappointed /ˌdɪsəˈpɔɪntɪd/ (adj) unhappy because you hoped for something that didn't happen, or that was not as good as you expected

CHAPTER 2

A Visit to Andover

*A strange feeling came over me as I looked down on that old face and thin grey hair.
She looked so peaceful, so distanced from any violent event.*

We were met at Andover by Inspector Glen, a tall, fair-haired man with a
pleasant smile. He gave us the facts about the case.

'The crime was discovered by Police **Constable** Dover at 1.00 am on the
morning of the 22nd. He noticed that the door of the shop wasn't locked. He
entered, and at first he thought that the place was empty. But when he shone a
light over the **counter**, he saw the body of the old woman.

'When the police doctor arrived, it was found that the woman had been hit
hard on the back of the head. The doctor said that she had probably died about
seven to nine hours earlier.

'But we've found a man who went in and bought some tobacco at 5.30,' said
Inspector Glen. 'And a second man went in and found the shop empty at five
minutes past six. So that puts the time of death at between 5.30 and 6.05.

'We haven't been able to find anyone yet who saw Ascher, the woman's
husband, near the shop at the time. But he was in a pub at nine o'clock and was
very drunk. He's not a very pleasant kind of man.'

'He didn't live with his wife?' asked Poirot.

'No. They separated some years ago. Ascher's German. He was a waiter at one
time, but he started drinking. After that, nobody wanted to employ him. His
wife worked as a cook-housekeeper to an old lady. When the woman died, she
left Mrs Ascher some money and Mrs Ascher started this tobacco and newspaper
business. Ascher used to come round and cause problems for her, so she gave him
a small amount of money every week to make him go away.'

'Had they any children?' asked Poirot.

'No. There's a niece. She's working as a **maid** near Overton.'

'And you say that this man Ascher used to **threaten** his wife?'

'That's right. He was terrible when he was drunk – threatening to kill her.'

'Was anything missing from the shop?' asked Poirot.

'Nothing. No money was taken. No signs of robbery.'

Constable /ˈkʌnstəbəl/ (n) an officer with a low position in the British police.
    The *Chief Constable* is an officer in charge of the police in a large area.
counter /ˈkaʊntə/ (n) the place in a shop where you are served, usually a long, flat
piece of furniture
maid /meɪd/ (n) a female servant, especially in a large house
threaten /ˈθretn/ (v) to say that you are going to hurt someone, or cause problems

'You think that this man Ascher came into the shop drunk, started threatening his wife and finally struck her down?'

'It seems the most likely solution,' said the Inspector. 'But I'd like to have another look at that letter you received. I was wondering if Ascher wrote it.'

Poirot handed over the letter and the Inspector read it.

'I don't think it's from Ascher,' he said at last. 'I don't think that he would use the words "our" British police. It's good quality paper, too. It's strange that the letter should say the 21st of the month. Of course it might be **coincidence**.'

'That is possible – yes,' said Poirot.

'But I don't like this kind of coincidence, Mr Poirot. A B C. Who could A B C be? We'll see if Mary Drower – that's Mrs Ascher's niece – can give us any help. It's a strange business.'

A constable came in. 'Yes, Briggs, what is it?'

'It's the man Ascher, sir. We've found him.'

'Right. Bring him in here. Where was he?'

'Hiding down by the railway.'

Franz Ascher was a very unattractive man. He was crying and threatening us at the same time. He looked at each of our faces in turn.

'What do you want with me? You should be ashamed to bring me here! You are pigs! How dare you do this?' His voice changed suddenly. 'No, no, I do not mean that – you would not hurt a poor old man – not be hard on him. Everyone is hard on poor old Franz. Poor old Franz.'

Mr Ascher started to cry.

'Stop that, Ascher,' said the Inspector. 'Control yourself. You're not in any trouble yet. If you didn't kill your wife ...'

Ascher interrupted him, his voice almost a scream.

'I did not kill her! I did not kill her! It is all lies! You are English pigs – all against me. I would never kill her – never.'

'You often threatened to kill her, Ascher.'

'No. You do not understand. That was just a joke between Alice and me.'

'A strange kind of joke! Where were you yesterday evening, Ascher?'

'I did not go near Alice. I was with friends – good friends. We were drinking at the Seven Stars – and then at the Red Dog. Dick Willows – he was with me – and old Curdie – and George – and Platt. It is the **truth** that I am telling you!'

'Take him away,' Inspector Glen said to Constable Briggs. 'Hold him on suspicion of murder. I don't know what to think,' he said as the unpleasant,

---

coincidence /kəʊˈɪnsɪdəns/ (n) a situation when two things happen at the same time or in the same place, in a surprising or unusual way

truth /truːθ/ (n) the true facts about something

shaking old man was taken out. 'If the letter didn't exist, I'd say he did it.'

'What about the men he talked about?' asked Poirot.

'A bad crowd – all ready to tell lies. But it's important to find out whether anyone saw him near the shop between half past five and six.'

Poirot shook his head thoughtfully.

'You are sure nothing was taken from the shop?' he asked.

'Perhaps a packet or two of cigarettes. But that's not a reason for murder.'

'And there was nothing – different about the shop? Nothing new there?'

'There was a railway guide,' said the Inspector. 'It was open and turned face down on the counter. It appeared that someone had looked up the trains from Andover. Either the old woman or a customer.'

'Did she sell that type of thing?' asked Poirot.

The Inspector shook his head.

'She sold cheap timetables. This was a big one – the kind of guide that only a big shop would sell.'

A light came into Poirot's eyes. He bent forward.

'A railway guide, you say. What kind? Was it an *ABC**?'

'Yes,' said the Inspector. 'It *was* an *ABC*.'

Until that moment, I had not felt very interested in the case. The murder of an old woman in a small back-street shop was a very ordinary type of crime. I had thought that the date of the 21st in the anonymous letter was just a coincidence. Mrs Ascher, I felt sure, had been murdered by her husband.

But now, when I heard about the railway guide, I felt a small shock of excitement. Surely – surely this could not be a second coincidence. The ordinary crime was turning into something very unusual.

We left the police station and went to the building where the body of the dead woman was being kept. A strange feeling came over me as I looked down on that old face and thin grey hair. She looked so peaceful, so distanced from any violent event.

'She was beautiful when she was young,' said Poirot.

'Really?' I said.

'But yes, look at the lines of the bones, the shape of the head.'

We went to see the police doctor, Dr Kerr.

'We haven't found what killed her,' he said. 'It's impossible to say what it was – perhaps a heavy stick.'

'Did the murderer have to be very strong?' asked Poirot.

'Do you mean, could the killer be a shaky old man of seventy? Oh, yes, it's

* an *ABC*: a guide to train times that first appeared in 1853

11

possible – if there was enough weight in the head of the stick.'

'Then the murderer could be a man or a woman?'

The doctor looked surprised.

'A woman, eh? I hadn't thought of connecting a woman with this type of crime. But of course it's possible.'

Poirot **nodded** in agreement. 'How was the body lying?' he asked.

'In my opinion, Mrs Ascher was standing with her back to the counter. The murderer hit her on the back of the head and she fell down behind the counter. So she couldn't be seen by anybody entering the shop.'

We thanked Dr Kerr and left.

'You see, Hastings,' said Poirot, 'this shows that Ascher may be innocent. A woman *faces* a man who is threatening her. But instead, she had her back to the murderer. So clearly she was taking down tobacco or cigarettes for a *customer*.'

Poirot looked at his watch. 'Overton is not far away. Shall we drive over there and have an interview with the niece of the dead woman?'

A few minutes later we were driving towards Overton.

Inspector Glen had given us the address of Mrs Ascher's niece. It was a big house about one and a half kilometres from the village, on the London side. The door was opened by a pretty dark-haired girl. Her eyes were red from crying.

'I think you are Miss Mary Drower, the maid here?' asked Poirot gently.

'Yes, sir, that's right. I'm Mary, sir.'

'Then perhaps I can talk to you for a few minutes. It's about your aunt.'

We went inside the house and Mary opened the door of a small living-room. We entered and Poirot sat down on a chair by the window. He looked up into the girl's face, studying it closely.

'You have heard of your aunt's death, of course?'

The girl nodded, tears filling her eyes again.

'This morning, sir. The police came here. Oh! it's terrible! Poor Auntie!'

'You were fond of your aunt, Mary?' said Poirot gently.

'Very, sir. She was always very good to me. I usually visited Auntie on my free day. She had a lot of trouble with her husband.'

'Tell me, Mary, did he threaten her?'

'Oh yes, sir. He used to say he would cut her throat, and things like that.'

'So you were not very surprised when you learned what had happened?'

'Oh, but I was,' Mary replied. 'You see, sir, I never thought that he meant it. And Auntie wasn't afraid of him. *He* was afraid of *her*.'

'Ah,' said Poirot. 'So, supposing someone else killed her ... Have you any idea who that person could be?'

nod /nɒd/ (v) to move your head up and down in understanding or agreement

'I've no idea, sir,' said Mary in great surprise. 'It doesn't seem likely.'

'There was no one that your aunt was afraid of?'

Mary shook her head. 'Auntie wasn't afraid of people.'

'Did she ever get anonymous letters? Letters that weren't signed – or were only signed with letters like A B C?'

Mary shook her head in surprise.

Poirot got up. 'If I want you at any time, Mary, I will write to you here.'

'Actually, sir, I'm going to leave this job. I don't like the country. I stayed here to be near my aunt. But now' – her eyes filled with tears again – 'there's no reason for me to stay, so I'll go back to London.'

'When you do go to London, will you give me your address?'

Poirot handed her his card. Mary looked at the card in surprise.

'Then you're not – a policeman, sir?'

'I am a private detective.'

She stood there looking at him for some moments in silence.

'Is there anything – strange happening, sir?'

'Yes, my child,' replied Poirot. 'There is something strange happening. Later you may be able to help me.'

'I – I'll do anything, sir. It – it isn't *right*, sir, Auntie being killed.'

It was a strange way to describe her aunt's death, but I felt full of pity.

A few moments later we were driving back to Andover.

2.1 Were you right?

Look at your answers to Activity 1.2 on page iv. Then correct these sentences.

1 Captain Hastings has known Hercule Poirot since his marriage.

....

2 Captain Hastings is afraid that the letter is from a murderer.

....

3 The dead woman's husband owns a tobacco and magazine shop.

....

4 Mrs Ascher sold expensive railway guides.

....

5 The doctor says that the murderer must be a man.

....

2.2 What more did you learn?

Use these words to complete the report below.

counter	checked	shone	guide	burglars	body	empty

POLICE REPORT   22 June, Andover

At about 1 a.m. on the morning of 22 June, I was walking past
Mrs Ascher's shop. Everything in the street looked quiet, but
I was worried about ¹............................... . So I ²...............................
the door of the shop to make sure it was locked. But the door
wasn't locked. I opened it and went inside. At first I thought the
place was ³............................... . But when I ⁴...............................
my light over the ⁵............................... , I saw the
⁶............................... of an old woman lying on the floor. While I
was waiting for the police doctor, I also noticed an <u>ABC</u> railway
⁷............................... turned face down on the counter.

Derrick Dover (Police Constable)

2.3 **Language in use**

Look at the sentences on the right.
Then complete the sentences below
with past perfect active or passive
forms of the verbs.

> He **had moved** to a new flat in London.
>
> Mrs Ascher, I felt sure, **had been murdered** by her husband.

1   The letter .... on good quality paper. (write)

2   Mrs Ascher .... many times by her husband.   (threaten)

3   According to Mr Ascher, he .... the evening with friends. (spend)

4   Mrs Ascher .... on the back of the head. (hit)

5   She .... her back to the murderer. (have)

6   Nothing .... from the shop. (take)

7   An *ABC* guide .... on the counter. (leave)

8   Poirot .... that the letter was not serious. (hope)

2.4 **What happens next?**

1   **What questions will Poirot ask Mrs Ascher's neighbours, do you think?**
    Write some below.

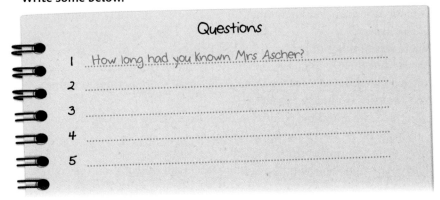

Questions

1   How long had you known Mrs Ascher?

2   ....

3   ....

4   ....

5   ....

2   **Look at the picture on page 23. What do you think?**

   a   Who is the letter to? ....

   b   Who is it from? ....

   c   What does it say? ....

   d   Why do Poirot and Hastings look worried? ....

CHAPTER 3

Questions and Answers

'Perhaps you even saw the murderer go into the shop –
a tall, fair man with a beard, was he not? A Russian, I have heard.'

The murder had taken place on a street which was a turning off the main street. Mrs Ascher's shop was about half-way down it on the right-hand side. A large crowd of people was standing outside the shop. A young constable was trying to make the crowd move away.

Poirot stopped at a little distance from them. From there we could see the sign over the shop door. Poirot repeated it softly.

'A. Ascher. Come, let us go inside, Hastings.'

We made our way through the crowd. Poirot showed the young constable a letter from Inspector Glen, explaining who we were. He nodded, and unlocked the door to let us pass inside.

The shop was very dark. The constable found and switched on the electric light. There were a few cheap magazines lying about, and newspapers from the day before – all dusty. Behind the counter there were shelves reaching to the ceiling, packed with tobacco and packets of cigarettes. There were also jars of sweets. It was an ordinary little shop, like thousands of others.

'She was down behind the counter,' the constable explained in a slow voice. 'The doctor says she never knew what hit her. She was probably reaching up to one of the shelves.'

'There was nothing in her hand?' asked Poirot.

'No, sir, but there was a packet of cigarettes down beside her.'

Poirot nodded. His eyes moved round the small shop, noting everything.

'And the railway guide was – where?'

'Here, sir.' The constable pointed out the place on the counter. 'It was open at the right page for Andover and lying face down.'

'Were there any fingerprints?' I asked.

'There were none on the railway guide, sir. There were lots on the counter itself.'

'Were there any of Ascher's among them?' asked Poirot.

'Too soon to say, sir.'

Poirot nodded again, then asked if the dead woman lived over the shop.

'Yes, sir, you go through that door at the back, sir.'

Poirot passed through the door and I followed him. Behind the shop there was a small room which was both a kitchen and living-room. It was tidy and clean but without much furniture. There were a few photographs on a shelf over the fire. One was of Mary Drower, Mrs Ascher's niece. Another was of a young couple in old-fashioned clothes. The girl looked beautiful and the young man was handsome.

'Probably a wedding picture,' said Poirot.

I looked closely at the couple in the photograph. It was almost impossible to recognise the well-dressed young man as Ascher.

Upstairs there were two more small rooms. One had been the dead woman's bedroom. There were a couple of old blankets on the bed; a small pile of underwear in one drawer and cookery books in another; a magazine; a pair of shiny new **stockings**, and a few clothes hanging up.

'Come, Hastings,' said Poirot quietly. 'There is nothing for us here.'

When we were out in the street again, Poirot crossed the road. Almost exactly opposite Mrs Ascher's shop, there was a shop selling fruit and vegetables. In a quiet voice, Poirot told me what I had to do. Then he entered the shop. After waiting a minute or two, I followed him in. He was buying some green beans. I chose some apples.

Poirot talked excitedly to the fat lady who was serving him.

'It was just opposite you, was it not, that the murder happened? Perhaps you even saw the murderer go into the shop – a tall, fair man with a beard, was he not? A Russian, I have heard.'

stocking /ˈstɒkɪŋ/ (n) a very thin piece of clothing that fits tightly over a woman's foot and leg

'What's that?' The woman looked up in surprise. 'A Russian did it?'

'*Mais oui*. I thought perhaps you noticed him last night?'

'Well, I don't get much chance to look,' said the woman. 'The evening's our busy time and there are always a lot of people passing after they finish work. A tall fair man with a beard – no, I can't say I saw him.'

I interrupted the conversation as Poirot had told me to.

'Excuse me, sir,' I said to Poirot. 'I think you have the wrong information. A short *dark* man, I was told.'

A discussion started between the fat woman, her husband and a young assistant. They had seen *four* short dark men, and the assistant had seen a tall fair one.

Poirot and I left the shop with our beans and apples.

'And why did you do that, Poirot?' I asked.

'I wanted to find out if it was possible for a stranger to enter Mrs Ascher's shop without being noticed.'

'Couldn't you simply ask those people if they saw anyone?'

'No, *mon ami*. If I asked those people for information, they would not tell me anything. But when I made a statement, they started to talk. We now know that this time is a "busy time" – there are a lot of people on the streets. Our murderer chose his time well, Hastings.'

We gave our beans and apples to a very surprised small boy in the street. Then Poirot paused and looked at the houses on each side of Mrs Ascher's house. One was a house with curtains that had been white but were now grey. Poirot knocked at the door. It was opened by a very dirty child.

'Good evening,' said Poirot. 'Is your mother in?'

The child stared at us for a long time. Then he shouted up the stairs.

'Mum, you're wanted.'

A sharp-faced woman came down the stairs.

'You're wasting your time here – ' she began, but Poirot interrupted her.

'Good evening, madam,' he said. 'I am a newspaper reporter, working for the *Evening Star*. I would like to offer you five pounds for some information about your neighbour, Mrs Ascher.'

As soon as Poirot talked about money, the woman became more pleasant.

'I'm sorry I spoke so crossly just now,' she said, 'but a lot of men come along and try to sell me things – cleaning products, stockings, bags and other silly things. They all seem to know my name, too – Mrs Fowler.'

'Well, Mrs Fowler,' said Poirot, 'you only have to give me some information. Then I'll write a report of the interview.'

Mrs Fowler began to talk about Mrs Ascher. She had had a lot of trouble with Franz Ascher. Everyone knew that. But she hadn't been afraid of him.

Had Mrs Ascher ever received any strange letters, Poirot asked – letters without a signature? Mrs Fowler didn't think so. Had Mrs Fowler seen a railway guide – an *ABC* – in Mrs Ascher's home? Mrs Fowler replied that she hadn't. Had anyone seen Ascher go into the shop the evening before? Again, Mrs Fowler said no.

Poirot paid her the five pounds and we went out into the street again.

'That was rather an expensive interview, Poirot,' I said. 'Do you think she knows more than she told us?'

'My friend, we are in the strange position of *not knowing what questions to ask*,' replied Poirot. 'Mrs Fowler has told us all that she *thinks* she knows. In the future, that information may be useful for us.'

I didn't understand what Poirot meant, but at that moment we met Inspector Glen. He was looking rather unhappy. He had spent the afternoon trying to get a list of people who had been seen entering the tobacco shop.

'And nobody has seen anyone?' asked Poirot.

'Oh, yes, they have. Three tall men, four short men with black moustaches, two beards, three fat men – all strangers, and all looking like criminals!'

Poirot smiled.

'Does anyone say that they have seen the man Ascher?'

'No, they don't. And that's another reason why he might be innocent. I've just told the Chief Constable that I think this is a job for Scotland Yard. I don't believe it's a local crime.'

Poirot said seriously, 'I agree with you.'

The Inspector said, 'You know, Monsieur Poirot, it's a nasty business – I don't like it ... '

We had two more interviews before returning to London.

The first was with Mr James Partridge, who had bought something from Mrs Ascher at 5.30.

Mr Partridge was a tidy little man. He worked in a bank and wore glasses on the end of his nose. He was very exact in everything he said.

'Mr – er – Poirot,' he said, looking at the card my friend had handed to him. 'From Inspector Glen? What can I do for you, Mr Poirot?'

'I understand that you were the last person to see Mrs Ascher alive?'

Mr Partridge placed the ends of his fingers together and stared at Poirot.

'That is not certain, Mr Poirot,' he said. 'It's possible that there were other customers after me.'

'If there were, they have not reported it,' said Poirot. 'But you, I understand, went to the police without waiting to be asked?'

'Certainly I did. As soon as I heard about the shocking event, I realised that my statement might be helpful.'

'You have an excellent sense of duty,' said Poirot. 'Perhaps you could kindly repeat your story to me.'

'Certainly. I was returning to this house and at 5.30 exactly I entered Mrs Ascher's shop. I often bought things there. It was on my way home.'

'Did you know that Mrs Ascher had a drunken husband who was in the habit of threatening her life?'

'No. I knew nothing about her.'

'Did you think there was anything unusual about her appearance yesterday evening? Did she seem different from usual?'

Mr Partridge thought for a time.

'She seemed exactly as usual,' he said at last.

Poirot got up.

'Thank you, Mr Partridge, for answering these questions. Have you an *ABC* in the house? I want to look up my return train to London.'

'On the shelf behind you,' said Mr Partridge.

Poirot took down the *ABC* and pretended to look up a train. Then he thanked Mr Partridge and we left.

Our next interview was with Mr Albert Riddell. Mr Riddell was an enormous man with a large face and small suspicious eyes.

He looked at us angrily.

'I've told everything once already,' he said. 'I've told the police, and now I've got to tell it again to two foreigners.'

Poirot gave me a quick, amused look, and then said, 'I am sorry, but it is a case of murder. One has to be very, very careful. You did not, I think, go to the police?'

'Why should I? It wasn't my business. I've got my work to do.'

'People saw you going into the shop and gave your name to the police. But the police had to come to you first. Were they happy with your information?'

'Why shouldn't they be?' said Mr Riddell angrily. 'Everyone knows who killed the old woman – that husband of hers.'

'But he was not in the street that evening and you were.'

'You're trying to say that I did it, are you? Well, you won't succeed. What reason did I have to do a thing like that?'

He got up from his chair in a threatening way.

'Calm yourself, monsieur,' said Poirot. 'I only want you to tell me about your visit. It was six o'clock when you entered the shop?'

'That's right – a minute or two after six. I wanted a packet of tobacco. I pushed open the door and went in. There wasn't anyone there. I waited, but nobody came so I went out again.'

'You didn't see the body behind the counter?'

'No.'

'Was there a railway guide lying about?'

'Yes, there was – face down. I thought perhaps the old woman had to go somewhere by train and forgot to lock the shop.'

'Perhaps you picked up the railway guide and moved it along the counter?'

'I didn't touch it. I did just what I said,' said Mr Riddell angrily.

'And you did not see anyone leaving the shop before you got there?'

'No. Why are you trying to fix this murder on me?'

Poirot got up.

'Nobody is fixing anything on you – yet. *Bon soir**, monsieur.'

Poirot went out into the street and I followed him. He looked at his watch.

'If we are quick, my friend, we might catch the 7.02 train to London.'

---

* *bon soir:* French for 'good evening'

CHAPTER 4

The Second Letter

Poirot turned to me with a worried face. 'Madness, Hastings, is a terrible thing ... I am afraid ... I am very much afraid ...'

We were seated in the fast train to London. The train had just left Andover. 'Well?' I asked Poirot in a hopeful voice.

'The murderer,' said Poirot, 'is a man of normal height with red hair. He has a problem with his right foot and he has a small mark on the skin just below his left shoulder.'

'Poirot!' I cried in surprise. How did my clever friend know so much about the murderer? Then I looked at him again. He had an amused look on his face.

'Poirot!' I said again, but this time I was disappointed.

'*Mon ami*, what do you want? You are expecting me to be like Sherlock Holmes*! But this is the truth – *I do not know what the murderer looks like, where he lives or how he can be found.*'

'It's a pity that he didn't leave a clue,' I said.

'Well, my friend, there is the *railway guide*. The *ABC*, that is a clue.'

'Do you think he left it by mistake?'

'Of course not. He left it on purpose. The fingerprints tell us that.'

'But there weren't any on it.'

'That is what I mean. Since there are no fingerprints on the *ABC*, it was carefully cleaned. So our murderer left it there for a purpose.'

Poirot continued slowly, 'We are faced here with an unknown person. In one way we know nothing about him. But in another way we know a lot about him. He has a typewriter and he buys good quality paper. And we can ask ourselves some useful questions. Why the *ABC*? Why Mrs Ascher? Why Andover?'

'The woman's past life seems simple enough,' I said thoughtfully. 'The interviews with those two men were disappointing. They couldn't tell us anything more than we knew already.'

'But there is a possibility that the murderer lives in or near Andover,' said Poirot. 'And these two men were in the shop when the murder took place. But, personally, Hastings, I think the murderer came from outside. And we must not forget that perhaps it was a woman. The method of attack is a man's. But anonymous letters are written by women more often than by men.'

I was silent for a few minutes, then I said. 'What do we do next?'

'Nothing,' said Poirot, smiling at me.

'Nothing?' Again, I heard the disappointment in my voice.

* Sherlock Holmes: a famous fictional detective

'Am I a magician? What do you want me to do? The police are doing everything they can. They will discover anything that can be discovered.'

In the days that followed, I found that Poirot was strangely unwilling to talk about the case. In my own mind, I was afraid that I knew the reason why.

Poirot hadn't been able to solve the murder of Mrs Ascher. My friend was used to success and he found failure very difficult – so difficult that he didn't even want to talk about it.

The crime received very little attention in the newspapers. There was nothing exciting or unusual about the murder of an old woman. The newspapers soon found more exciting subjects to write about.

I was beginning to forget about the matter when something new happened. I hadn't seen Poirot for a couple of days as I had been away for the weekend. I arrived back on the Monday afternoon and the letter came by the six o'clock post. Poirot opened the envelope and breathed in deeply.

'It has come,' he said.

'What has come?'

'The second part of the ABC business. Read it,' said Poirot, and passed me the letter.

As before, it was typed on good quality paper.

Dear Mr Poirot, Well, I won the first part of the game, I think. The Andover business went very well, didn't it?

But the fun's only just beginning. Watch what happens at Bexhill-on-Sea on the 25th of the month. What a great time we are having!

Yours, A B C

◆

'Does this mean this man is going to try and murder someone else?' I said.

'Naturally, Hastings. Did you think that the Andover business was going to be the only case? Do you not remember me saying, "This is the beginning"?'

'But this is horrible! We're facing a mad killer.'

The next morning there was a meeting of some powerful police officials. There was the Chief Constable of Sussex, Inspector Glen from Andover, **Superintendent** Carter of the Sussex police, Inspector Japp, a younger inspector called Crome, and also Dr Thomson, the famous specialist in illnesses of the mind. Everyone was sure that the two letters were written by the same person.

'We've now got definite warning of a second crime, which is going to take place on the 25th – the day after tomorrow – in Bexhill. What can we do to stop it?' said the Sussex Chief Constable. He looked at his superintendent.

The Superintendent shook his head. 'It's difficult, sir. There's not the smallest clue about who the **victim** will be. What *can* we do?'

'I have a suggestion,' said Poirot. 'I think it is possible that the surname of the intended victim will begin with the letter B. When I got the letter naming Bexhill, I thought it was possible that the victim as well as the place might be chosen in **alphabetical** order.'

'It's possible,' said the doctor. 'On the other hand, it may be that the name Ascher was a coincidence. Remember that we are facing a madman. He hasn't given us any clue about his **motive**.'

'Does a madman *have* motives, sir?' asked the Superintendent.

'Of course he does,' said the doctor.

'I'll keep a special watch on anyone connected with the Andover business,' said Inspector Glen. 'Partridge and Riddell and, of course, Ascher himself. If they show any sign of leaving Andover, they'll be followed.'

Later, Poirot and I walked along by the river.

'Poirot,' I said. 'Surely this crime can be stopped?'

Poirot turned to me with a worried face. 'Madness, Hastings, is a terrible thing ... I am afraid ... I am very much afraid ...'

Superintendent /ˌsuːpərɪnˈtendənt/ (n) a British police officer with an important position
victim /ˈvɪktɪm/ (n) someone who has been attacked, killed or murdered
alphabetical /ˌælfəˈbetɪkəl/ (adj) arranged in order from A–Z
motive /ˈməʊtɪv/ (n) the reason for someone's actions, especially bad ones

I still remember waking up on the morning of 25 July. It was about seven-thirty. Poirot was standing by my bedside, gently shaking me by the shoulder. I looked at his face and was awake at once.

'What is it?' I asked, sitting up quickly.

'*It has happened*,' Poirot said.

'What?' I cried. 'You mean – but *today* is the 25th.'

'It took place last night – I mean, in the early hours of this morning.'

I jumped out of bed and got dressed quickly. Poirot had just had a telephone call from Bexhill-on-Sea. He told me what had happened.

'The body of a young girl has been found on the beach at Bexhill,' he said. 'She is Elizabeth Barnard, a waitress in one of the cafés. According to the medical examination, the time of death was between 11.30 p.m. and 1 a.m. *An ABC open at the trains to Bexhill was found under the body.*'

Twenty minutes later we were in a fast car crossing the Thames on our way out of London. Inspector Crome was with us. He was officially in charge of the case. Crome was a very different type of officer from Japp. He was much younger, and seemed to think that he was a better detective than Poirot.

'If you want to ask me anything about the case, please do,' he said.

'You have not, I suppose, a description of the dead girl?' asked Poirot.

'She was twenty-three years old and was working as a waitress at the

Orange Cat café – '

'*Pas ça**. I wondered – if she was pretty?'

'I have no information about that,' said Inspector Crome rather coldly.

A look of amusement came into Poirot's eyes.

'It does not seem to you important? But for a woman, it is very important!'

There was a short silence. Then Poirot opened the conversation again.

'Were you informed how the girl was murdered?'

'She was **strangled** with her own belt,' replied Inspector Crome.

Poirot's eyes opened very wide.

'Ah!' he said. 'At last we have a piece of information that is very definite. That tells one something, does it not?'

At Bexhill we were greeted by Superintendent Carter. With him was a pleasant-faced, intelligent-looking young inspector called Kelsey.

'We've told the girl's mother and father about her death,' said the Superintendent. 'It was a terrible shock to them, of course. There's also a sister – a typist in London. We've communicated with her. And there's a young man – in fact, the girl was supposed to be out with him last night.'

'Any help from the *ABC* guide?' asked Crome.

'It's there.' The Superintendent nodded towards the table. 'No fingerprints. It's open at the page for Bexhill. It's a new book, I think – it hasn't been opened much. It wasn't bought anywhere round here.'

'Who discovered the body, sir?'

'A retired army officer who was walking his dog at about 6 a.m.'

'Well, sir, I'd better start the interviews,' said Crome. 'There's the café and the girl's home. I'd better go to both of them. Kelsey can come with me.'

'And Mr Poirot?' asked the Superintendent.

'I will go with you,' said Poirot to Crome.

Crome, I thought, looked a little annoyed.

We went to the Orange Cat, a small tearoom by the sea. It served coffee, tea and a few lunch dishes. Coffee was just being served. The manageress took us into a very untidy back room.

'Miss – eh – Merrion?' asked Crome.

'That is my name,' said the manageress in a high voice. 'This is a very upsetting business. Most upsetting.'

'What can you tell me about the dead girl, Miss Merrion?' asked Kelsey. 'Had she worked here for a long time?'

'This was the second summer. She was a good waitress.'

---

* *pas ça*: French for 'not that'

strangle /ˈstræŋgəl/ (v) to kill someone by pressing their neck or pulling something tight around it

'She was pretty, yes?' asked Poirot.

'She was a nice, clean-looking girl,' replied Miss Merrion.

'What time did she finish work last night?' Poirot continued.

'Eight o'clock. We close at eight.'

'Did she tell you how she was going to spend the evening?'

'Certainly not,' said Miss Merrion. She looked shocked.

'How many waitresses do you employ?'

'Two normally, and an extra two from 20 July until the end of August. Miss Barnard was one of the regular waitresses.'

'What about the other one?'

'Miss Higley? She's a very nice young lady.'

'Perhaps we had better ask her some questions.'

'I'll send her to you,' said Miss Merrion. 'Please be as quick as possible. This is the busiest time for morning coffees.'

Miss Merrion left the room. A few minutes later a rather fat girl with dark hair and a pink face came in.

'Miss Higley,' asked the Inspector, 'you knew Elizabeth Barnard?'

'Oh, yes, I knew Betty. Isn't it *awful*? Betty! Betty Barnard, *murdered*!'

'You knew the dead girl well?' asked Crome.

'Well, she's worked here longer than I have. I only came this March. She was here last year. She was rather quiet. She didn't joke or laugh a lot.'

We learned that Betty Barnard had had a good-looking, well-dressed 'friend' who worked in an office near the station. Miss Higley didn't know his name, but she had seen him and she thought Miss Barnard had planned to meet him the night before. We talked to the other two girls in the café, but no one had noticed her in Bexhill during the evening.

3.1 Were you right?

Look at your answers to Activity 2.4. Then read the notes below. Poirot has interviewed four people about Mrs Ascher's death and made notes. Match the notes with the right people (a–d).

shopkeeper

Mrs Fowler

Mr Partridge

Mr Riddell

1 Didn't see Ascher go into the shop.   b
2 Didn't know Mrs A had a drunken husband.   ....
3 Went into the shop just after 6 p.m.   ....
4 Didn't meet anyone leaving the shop.   ....
5 Said Mrs A not afraid of her husband.   ....
6 Went into the shop at 5.30 p.m.   ....
7 Said Mrs A had problems with her husband.   ....
8 Went into Mrs A's shop to buy tobacco.   ....
9 Saw the ABC guide in the shop.   ....
10 Too busy to notice who went into the shop.   ....
11 Didn't notice that Mrs A had an ABC guide.   ....
12 Didn't notice anything unusual about Mrs A.   ....

3.2 What more did you learn?

Put these events in the right order. The first has been done for you.

a Poirot and Hastings go to the Orange Cat.   ☐
b Poirot and Hastings return to London.   1
c The body of a young girl is found.   ☐
d Poirot interviews Miss Merrion and Miss Higley.   ☐
e There is a meeting of important police officers.   ☐
f Poirot and Hastings travel to Bexhill.   ☐
g Poirot receives a second letter.   ☐

3.3 Language in use

Look at the sentence in the box.
Then complete Poirot's thoughts.

> If I **asked** those people for information,
> they **would not tell** me anything.

> But Poirot,
> who *is* A B C?

> I have no idea,
> *mon ami*!

1

If the police .... who the
anonymous letter writer ...., they
.... the murderer. (know, be, find)

2

Ascher .... away
if he .... the
murderer. (run, be)

3

If we .... the
murderer, we ....
the next victim. (find, save)

4

Crome .... a lot if
he .... to me
more carefully. (learn, listen)

5

If I .... a fortune-
teller, I ....
Hastings's questions! (be, answer)

3.4 What happens next?

1 Read the title of Chapter 5 on page 30 and the words in *italics* below it.
   Discuss these questions.

   a Who is the speaker talking about?
   b Who is the speaker? How is he or she feeling?

2 Read the title of Chapter 6 on page 36 and the words in *italics* below it.
   What do you think?

   a Who are the speakers?
   b What has happened just before this conversation?

A Broken Family

'Betty was just a happy girl with a nice boyfriend. Why should anyone want to murder her? It doesn't make sense.'

Elizabeth Barnard's parents lived in a small newly built house on the edge of the town. Mr Barnard was waiting in the doorway for us.

Inspector Kelsey introduced himself, then he introduced us.

'This is Inspector Crome of Scotland Yard, sir,' he said.

'Scotland Yard?' said Mr Barnard hopefully. 'That's good. This murderer has got to be caught. My poor little girl – '

'And this is Mr Hercule Poirot, also from London, and er – '

'Captain Hastings,' said Poirot.

We went into the living-room. Mrs Barnard was there. Her eyes were red, and she was clearly suffering from shock.

'It's too cruel. Oh, it is too cruel,' she said in a tearful voice.

'It's very painful for you, madam, I know,' said Inspector Crome. 'But we want to know all the facts so we can get to work as quickly as possible. Your daughter was twenty-three, I understand. She lived here with you and worked at the Orange Cat café, is that right?'

'That's it,' said Mr Barnard.

'This is a new house, isn't it? Where did you live before?'

'I worked in London. I retired two years ago. We always wanted to live near the sea.'

'You have two daughters?'

'Yes. My older daughter works in an office in London.'

'Weren't you worried when your daughter didn't come home last night?'

'We didn't know she hadn't,' said Mrs Barnard in a tearful voice. 'Dad and I always go to bed at nine o'clock. We never knew Betty hadn't come home until the police officer came and said – and said – ' She started to cry.

'We heard that your daughter was going to be married?'

'Yes. His name is Donald Fraser and I like him,' said Mrs Barnard. 'I like him very much. This news will be terrible for him.'

'Did he meet your daughter most evenings after her work?'

'Not every evening. Once or twice a week.'

'Do you know if she was going to meet him yesterday?'

'She didn't say. Betty never said much about where she was going or what she was doing. But she was a good girl, Betty was.'

'We've got to find out what happened,' said Mr Barnard. 'Betty was just

I felt sorry for the young man. His white face showed how great a shock he had had. He was a fine-looking young man with a pleasant face and red hair.

'What's this, Megan?' he said. 'Tell me, please – I've only just heard – Betty ...' His voice grew quieter.

Poirot pushed forward a chair and he sank down on it. Poirot gave him a drink. He sat up straighter and turned to Megan.

'It's true, I suppose?' he said quietly. 'Betty is – dead – killed?'

'It's true, Don. I've just come down from London. Dad phoned me. The police are upstairs now. Looking through Betty's things, I suppose.'

Poirot moved forward a little and asked a question.

'Did Miss Barnard tell you where she was going last night?'

'She told me she was going with a girlfriend to St Leonards,' replied Fraser.

'Did you believe her?' asked Poirot.

'What do you mean?' Suddenly Fraser's face looked angry.

'Betty Barnard was killed by a madman,' said Poirot. 'You can only help us to catch him by speaking the exact truth.'

Donald Fraser turned to Megan. Then he looked suspiciously at Poirot.

'Who are you? You don't belong to the police?'

'I am better than the police,' said Poirot simply.

'Well,' Donald Fraser said at last, 'I – I began to wonder. I was ashamed of myself for being so suspicious. But – but I was suspicious ... I went to St Leonards. I got there by eight o'clock. Then I watched the buses – to see if she was in them ... But there was no sign of her.

'I was sure she was with a man. I went to Hastings. I looked in hotels and restaurants and cinemas. It was very foolish. So in the end I came back. It was about midnight when I got home.'

The kitchen door opened.

'Oh, there you are,' said Inspector Kelsey.

Inspector Crome pushed past him. He looked quickly at the two strangers.

'Miss Megan Barnard and Mr Donald Fraser,' said Poirot, introducing them. 'This is Inspector Crome from London.' Turning to the Inspector, he said, 'While you were upstairs, I was talking to Miss Barnard and Mr Fraser to see if they could tell me anything which would help us.'

'Oh yes?' said Inspector Crome, not really listening to Poirot.

Poirot went out into the hall and I followed him.

'Have you had any new ideas about the crimes?' I asked him.

'Only that the murderer is a surprisingly kind sort of person,' said Poirot.

I had no idea what Poirot meant. But I did not say anything.

CHAPTER 6

The Third Letter

'This murder is worse because it's mad.'
'No, Hastings. It is not worse. It is only more difficult.'

After the Bexhill murder, we had many more meetings with the police. There was a lot of discussion about whether the general public should be told about the anonymous letters.

'If we don't give this madman the satisfaction of telling everyone about him, what's he likely to do?' asked Inspector Crome.

'He'll murder someone else,' said Dr Thomson at once.

'And if we put everything in the newspapers, then what will he do?'

'Same answer. The result's the same. Another crime.'

'But it seems to me,' said Poirot, 'that there is one very important clue – the discovery of the motive. He chooses his victims alphabetically – not because he hates them personally. But *why* is he murdering these people?'

'He is a very kind murderer. The police didn't **arrest** Franz Ascher for the murder of his wife and Donald Fraser for the murder of Betty Barnard because A B C wrote those warning letters.'

I remember well the arrival of A B C's third letter.

It was a Friday. The evening post came at about ten o'clock. When we heard the postman's step, I went along to the letter-box. There were four or five letters, I remember. The last one was addressed in printed letters.

I opened it quickly and took out the printed piece of paper inside.

Poor Mr Poirot, – You aren't as good at these little criminal matters as you thought, are you? Let us see if you can do any better this time. This time it's easy. Churston on the 30th. Do try and do something about it. It's a bit boring for me when everything goes so easily, you know!

Good hunting. Ever yours,
A B C

'Churston,' I said, jumping to get our own *ABC*. 'Let's see where it is.'

'Hastings,' said Poirot, 'when was that letter written? Is there a date on it?'

'It was written on the 27th,' I said, looking at the letter in my hand.

'Did I hear you right, Hastings? Did he give the date of the murder as the *30th? Bon Dieu**, Hastings – do you not realise? Today is the 30th.'

---

* *Bon Dieu:* French for 'Good God'

arrest /ə'rest/ (v) to take someone away to a police station because they are thought to be a criminal

Poirot picked up the envelope from the floor. There was something unusual about the address, but I had been too worried to look at it closely.

Poirot was at that time living in Whitehaven Apartments. The address on the envelope said, *Hercule Poirot, Whitehorse Apartments*. Someone had written across the envelope, *'Not known at Whitehorse Apartments, ECI, – try Whitehaven Apartments.'*

So the letter had been sent to the wrong address three days before.

'Quickly!' said Poirot. 'We must get in touch with Scotland Yard.'

He telephoned Crome and told him about the letter. Crome then put down the phone to book a ticket to Churston.

'It is too late,' said Poirot. He looked at the clock. 'It's twenty past ten. There is only another hour and forty minutes.'

I opened the railway guide I had taken down from the shelf.

'Churston, Devon,' I read, '327.6 kilometres from Paddington. Population 656. It's a small place. Surely our man would be noticed there.'

'But another person will be dead,' said Poirot. 'What time are the trains? I imagine that a train will be quicker than a car.'

'There's a midnight train from Paddington – it gets to Churston at 7.15.'

'We will take that, Hastings.'

I put a few things into a suitcase while Poirot again rang up Scotland Yard. A few minutes later, he came into the bedroom and explained that we had to take the letter and envelope to Paddington with us. Someone from Scotland Yard would meet us there.

When we arrived on the platform, we saw Inspector Crome.

'We don't have any news yet,' he said. 'All persons whose names begin with C are being warned by phone if possible. Where's the letter?'

Poirot gave it to him and he examined it.

'You don't think,' I suggested, 'that he put the wrong address on purpose?'

'No,' said Crome, shaking his head. 'The man's got his rules – crazy rules – and he keeps to them. He gives us warning.'

The Inspector, we found, was travelling by the same train. Just as the train was leaving the station, we saw a man running down the platform. He reached the Inspector's window and called up something. Poirot and I hurried down the train.

'You have news – yes?' asked Poirot.

Crome said quietly, 'It's very bad. Sir Carmichael Clarke has been found murdered.'

Sir Carmichael Clarke was quite famous. He had been a throat specialist but had retired. He was rich and owned one of the best-known collections of Chinese

art. He was married but had no children, and lived in a house he had built for himself near the Devon coast.

'*Eh bien**,' said Poirot. 'The whole country will look for A B C.'

'Unfortunately,' I said, 'that's what he wants.'

'True. But he may become careless ...'

'How strange all this is, Poirot,' I said. 'Do you know, this is the first crime of this kind that you and I have worked on together? All our murders have been – well, *private* murders. This murder is worse because it's *mad*.'

'No, Hastings. It is not worse. It is only more *difficult*. It should be easier to discover *because* it is mad. This alphabetical business ... If I could understand the idea – then everything would be clear and simple. These crimes must not continue.

* *Eh bien*: French for 'well'

Soon, soon, I must see the truth … Go, Hastings. Get some sleep. There will be a lot to do tomorrow.'

Churston is near the town of Torquay. Until about ten years ago there was only countryside around it, but recently small houses and new roads had appeared. Sir Carmichael Clarke had bought land with an open view of the sea and built a house. It was modern, and not large, but quite attractive.

A local police officer, Inspector Wells, met us at the station and told us what had happened. Sir Carmichael Clarke, it seemed, had been in the habit of taking a walk after dinner every evening. But at some time after eleven, he had still not returned. It was not long before his body was discovered. He had been hit on the back of the head with something heavy. *An open ABC had been placed face down on the dead body.*

We arrived at Combeside, Sir Carmichael's house, at about eight o'clock. The door was opened by a manservant. His hands were shaking and he looked very upset.

'Good morning, Deveril,' said the police officer. 'These are the gentleman from London.'

'This way, gentlemen,' said Deveril. He showed us into a long dining-room where breakfast was laid. 'I'll get Mr Franklin.'

A minute later, a big, fair-haired man with a sunburnt face entered the room. This was Franklin Clarke, the dead man's only brother. Inspector Wells introduced us to him. Franklin Clarke shook hands with each of us in turn.

'Let me offer you some breakfast,' he said. 'We can talk as we eat.'

We ate the excellent breakfast and drank coffee.

'Inspector Wells told me everything last night,' said Franklin Clarke. 'Is it really right, Inspector Crome, that my poor brother is the victim of a mad killer, that this is the third murder, and that, *in each case, an ABC railway guide has been left beside the body?*'

'That's right, Mr Clarke.'

'But why? What possible advantage can there be for the murderer?'

'It won't help us if we look for motives now, Mr Clarke,' said Inspector Crome. 'We need a few facts. Your brother was the same as usual yesterday? He received no unexpected letter – nothing to upset him?'

'No, he was quite as usual.'

'Not upset or worried in any way?'

'Excuse me, Inspector, I didn't say that. It was normal for my poor brother to be upset and worried. You may not know that his wife, Lady Clarke, is in very bad health. She is suffering from a terrible illness and will not live for long. My brother is very worried about her. I returned from the East not long ago and I was shocked at the change in him.'

'Imagine, Mr Clarke, that you found your brother shot – with a gun beside him. What would you think?' asked Poirot.

'I would think that he killed himself,' said Clarke.

'But he *didn't* kill himself,' said Crome. 'Now I believe, Mr Clarke, that it was your brother's habit to go for a walk every evening?'

'Quite right. He always did.'

'I suppose a stranger would be easily noticed around here?'

'No, in August many tourists come here in cars and buses and on foot – unfortunately. You've no idea how beautiful and peaceful this part of the world is in June and at the beginning of July.'

'Did any stranger come to the house and ask for Sir Carmichael yesterday?'

'Not that I know of – but we'll ask Deveril.'

He rang the bell and put the question to the manservant.

'No, sir, no one came to see Sir Carmichael.'

As Deveril left the room, a young woman came in.

'This is Miss Thora Grey,' said Franklin Clarke. 'My brother's secretary.'

The girl was very fair. She had the very fair hair and light grey eyes that one finds among Norwegians and Swedes. She looked about twenty-seven. Clarke brought her a cup of coffee, but she refused any food.

'Did you see the letters that Sir Carmichael received?' asked Crome. 'I suppose he never received a letter or letters signed A B C?'

'A B C?' She shook her head. 'No, I'm sure he didn't.'

'He didn't say he had noticed anyone during his evening walks recently? Have you yourself noticed any strangers?'

'No. Of course there are a lot of people here at this time of year.'

Inspector Crome asked to be shown the path of Sir Carmichael's nightly walk. Franklin Clarke led the way and we followed.

◆

Thora Grey and I were walking a little behind the others.

'I expect this has been a terrible shock to his wife,' I said.

'Lady Clarke is usually drugged. She doesn't know what's happening for a lot of the time,' replied Miss Grey.

We went out through the garden gate, and then along a small path leading down to the sea. Suddenly we came out to a place covered with grass which looked out over a beach of white stones. All around it dark green trees ran down to the sea. It was a beautiful place – white, deep-green and bright blue.

'This was my brother's evening walk,' said Clarke. 'He came here, then back up the path. Then he went across the fields back to the house.'

We continued and came to a place near some trees, half-way across the field where the body had been found.

'The murderer probably stood here in the shadow,' said Crome. 'Your brother almost certainly noticed nothing until he was struck down.'

We went back to the house. As we climbed up the stairs, the doctor came out of a room where the body had been taken, with a black bag in his hand.

'It's a very simple case,' he said. 'He didn't suffer. Death happened immediately. I'll just go and see Lady Clarke.'

A hospital nurse came out of another room, and the doctor joined her. We went to look at Sir Carmichael's body, and came out again quickly.

Miss Grey was standing at the head of the stairs. She looked upset.

'Miss Grey – ' I stopped. 'Is anything the matter?'

'I was thinking,' she said, 'about D. About the next murder. Something must be done. It has to be stopped.'

Clarke came out of a room behind me. 'What has to be stopped, Thora?'

'These awful murders.'

'Yes. I want to talk to Monsieur Poirot some time ... Is Crome any good?'

I replied that he was supposed to be a very clever officer.

'He has the look of a man who knows everything,' said Clarke, 'but what *does* he know? Nothing. I've got a plan. But we'll talk about that later.'

He knocked at the door where the doctor had entered.

Miss Grey was still staring in front of her.

'What are you thinking, Miss Grey?' I asked.

'I'm wondering *where he is now* ... the murderer, I mean.'

She went downstairs. I stood there thinking about her words.

A B C ... *Where was he now ...?*

4.1 Were you right?

Think back to your answers to Activity 3.4.

1 Match these descriptions with the pictures below (A–D).

    a Poirot and Hastings travel to Churston. ....

    b A third letter arrives for Poirot. ....

    c Poirot examines the scene of the crime. ....

    d A breakfast meeting with Sir Franklin Clarke. ....

2 Put the pictures in the right order (1–4).

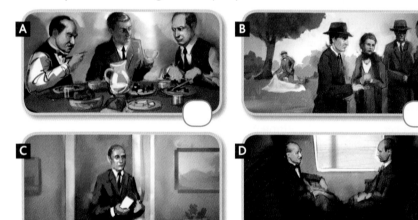

4.2 What more did you learn?

Read possible questions from Poirot. Who might they be for? Match each one with the right person.

1 Has something else happened, Inspector?	Megan Barnard
2 Was your brother upset about anything?	Donald Fraser
3 How long have you worked for Sir Carmichael?	Crome
4 Did your sister have any men friends?	Franklin Clarke
5 How frequent are the trains to Churston?	Thora Grey
6 Did Miss Barnard go out with you last night?	Hastings

4.3 Language in use

Look at the sentence in the box. Then complete these sentences with *so* + adjective + *that*.

> Don was **so violent that** Betty was frightened.

1 Mrs Ascher's shop was .... Poirot and Hastings could not see anything.

2 Ascher was .... he could not speak sensibly or walk in a straight line.

3 Poirot was .... the police often asked him for help.

4 Betty Barnard was .... a lot of men wanted to go out with her.

5 Poirot and Hastings were .... they ate a large breakfast.

6 A B C was .... Poirot could not catch him.

7 Thora Grey's hair was .... people thought she was Swedish.

4.4 What happens next?

Look at the picture and answer the questions.

1 Who is the man reading the newspaper?

....

....

2 What is he reading about?

....

....

3 What is the young man saying?

....

....

The Special Legion

'Only one thing connects these three people –
the fact that the same person killed them.'

M r Alexander Bonaparte Cust left the cinema in Torquay with the rest of the people. He looked around him uncertainly in the brightness of the afternoon sunshine, like a lost dog.

Newsboys went past, shouting: 'Latest news ... Mad Killer at Churston ...'

Mr Cust found a coin in his pocket, and bought a paper. He entered the Princess Gardens and sat down. Then he opened the paper.

There were big headlines:

SIR CARMICHAEL CLARKE MURDERED.

TERRIBLE EVENT AT CHURSTON.

WORK OF A MAD KILLER.

Only a month ago England was shocked by the murder of a young girl, Elizabeth Barnard, at Bexhill. It may be remembered that an ABC railway guide was found beside the body. An ABC was also found by the dead body of Sir Carmichael Clarke. The police think the same person is responsible for both murders. Is it possible that a mad killer is going round our seaside towns?

A young man in a bright blue shirt was sitting beside Mr Cust.

'A nasty business – eh?' he said.

Mr Cust jumped in surprise. 'Oh, very – very – '

The young man noticed that his hands were shaking so much that he couldn't hold the paper very well.

44

'Mad people don't always look mad,' said the young man. 'Often they seem just like you or me ... Sometimes it's the war that made them go mad.'

'I – I expect you're right.'

'I don't agree with wars,' said the young man. 'They should be stopped.'

Mr Cust laughed. He laughed for some time. The young man was worried.

'He's a bit mad himself,' he thought.

'Sorry, sir,' he said. 'I expect you were in the war.'

'I was,' said Mr Cust. 'My head's never been right since. It aches, you know. It aches terribly. Sometimes I don't know what I'm doing ...'

The young man went away quickly. Mr Cust stayed with his paper. He read it and read it again. People passed backwards and forwards in front of him. Most of them were talking about the murder.

'– police are sure to get him – '

'– say he may be arrested at any time now – '

'– quite likely he's in Torquay – '

Mr Cust laid the paper on the seat. Then he got up and walked towards the town. Girls passed him, girls in white and pink and blue. They laughed, looking at the men as they passed them.

But they didn't look once at Mr Cust.

He sat down at a little table and ordered tea.

After the murder of Sir Carmichael Clarke, the ABC murders were in every newspaper. The Andover murder was now connected with the other two. Scotland Yard believed that the best chance of catching the murderer was to make the murders as public as possible. The population of Great Britain turned into private detectives, looking for the murderer. One newspaper wrote:

HE MAY BE IN *YOUR* TOWN!

The newspapers printed the letters that had been sent to Poirot. Newspaper reporters kept asking Poirot for interviews. Scotland Yard were very active, working hard to check the smallest clues. They questioned people in hotels and guesthouses. They listened to hundreds of stories from imaginative people and checked them to see if they were true.

But Poirot seemed to me strangely inactive. Sometimes we argued.

'But what do you want me to do, my friend?' Poirot said. 'The police can question people better than I can. All the time, while I seem to be doing nothing, I am thinking – not about the facts of the case – but about the mind of the murderer.'

'The mind of a madman!'

'Exactly. *When I know what the murderer is like, I shall be able to find out who he is.* And all the time, I learn more. After the next crime – '

'Poirot!'

'But, yes, Hastings, I think it is almost certain there will be another crime. Our unknown killer has been lucky, but this time his luck may change. And after another crime, we shall know a lot more. I shall not know his name and address! But I shall know *what kind of a man he is ...*

'Now I am going to do something which will please you,' Poirot continued. 'It will mean a lot of conversation. I want to find out more information from the friends, relatives and servants of the victims.'

'Do you suspect them of hiding things?'

'I don't think they *meant* to hide information. But at the time of a murder, people talk about only what they *think* is important. Quite often they think wrong! And by discussing a certain event, or a certain person, again and again, they may remember extra details.'

It did not seem to me to be a very good idea.

'You do not agree with me?' said Poirot. 'Then a servant girl is cleverer than you.'

He handed me a letter. It was clearly written.

Dear Sir, – I hope you don't mind me writing to you. I have been thinking a lot since those awful two murders like poor auntie's. I saw the young lady's picture in the paper, the sister of the young lady who was killed at Bexhill. I wrote to her to tell her I was coming to London and asked if I could come to her. Perhaps if we talked about it together, we might find out something.

The young lady wrote back to me and suggested I might write to you. She said she'd been thinking the same. She said we ought to work together. So I'm coming to London, and this is my address.

Yours
Mary Drower

'Mary Drower,' said Poirot, 'is a very intelligent girl.'

He picked up another letter. It was a note from Franklin Clarke, saying that he was coming to London. He would visit Poirot the following day.

'Do not worry, *mon ami*,' said Poirot. 'There will be action.'

Franklin Clarke arrived at three o'clock on the following afternoon.

'Monsieur Poirot,' he said, 'I'm still not satisfied. I'm sure that Crome is a very good officer, but he annoys me. He seems to think he knows best! My idea is, Monsieur Poirot, that we mustn't delay. We've got to get ready for the next crime. I suggest that we form a kind of special **legion** – of the friends and relatives of the murdered people.

legion /'liːdʒən/ (n) a large group of soldiers, especially in the Roman army

'If we talk about things together, we might be able to find out something new. Also, when the next warning comes, one of us might recognise somebody who was near the scene of an earlier crime.

'My brother was a rich man and he left me some money. I can pay for everything. So I suggest the members of the special legion are paid for their services the same way as in a normal job. I suggest myself, Miss Barnard and Mr Donald Fraser, who was planning to marry the dead girl. Then there is a niece of the Andover woman – Miss Barnard knows her address.'

'Nobody else?'

'Well – er – Miss Grey.' As he spoke her name, Franklin Clarke suddenly looked much younger. He looked like a shy schoolboy. 'Yes. You see, Miss Grey worked for my brother for over two years. She knows the countryside and the people round there. I've been away for a year and a half in China, looking for things for my brother's art collection.'

'Very interesting,' said Poirot. 'Well, Mr Clarke, I agree with your idea.'

A few days later, the 'Special Legion' met at Poirot's rooms. Each of the three girls was attractive in a different way – the fair beauty of Thora Grey, the dark looks of Megan Barnard, and Mary Drower with her pretty, intelligent face. The two men were also very different. Franklin Clarke was big and talked a lot, and Donald Fraser was very quiet.

Poirot made a little speech.

'Here we have three murders – an old woman, a young girl, an older man. Only one thing connects these three people – *the fact that the same person killed them*. This means that *the same person was present in three different places* and was seen by a large number of people. He is a madman, but he does not look like one.

'But he did not murder his victims by chance. He chose them on purpose. And he spent time finding out about the places where they lived before the murders. I refuse to believe that there is no clue which can help us find out who he is. One of you – or possibly *all* of you – *knows something that they do not know they know*.'

'Words!' said Megan Barnard. 'It's just words. It doesn't mean anything.'

'Well, I think it's a good idea,' said Mary Drower. 'When you're talking about things, you often seem to understand more clearly.'

Poirot asked everyone in turn to tell the others what they remembered of the time before the murder. First Franklin Clarke spoke, and then Thora Grey, about Sir Carmichael Clarke's last day. Next, Megan Barnard and Donald Fraser talked about Betty Barnard. Finally Mary Drower spoke about the last letter she had received from her aunt.

'She said she wanted me to go to see her on my free day – and she said we'd go to the cinema. It was going to be my birthday, sir.' Suddenly Mary started to cry. 'You must forgive me, sir. I don't want to be silly. Crying's no good. It was the thought of her – and me – looking forward to our day out.'

'I know just how you feel,' said Franklin Clarke. 'It's always the little things that upset you – like remembering a present, or something fun.'

Megan said with a sudden warmth, 'That's true. The same thing happened after Betty died. Mum had bought some stockings for her as a present – bought them the same day it happened. Poor mum, she was so upset. I found her crying over them. She kept saying – "I bought them for Betty – and she never even saw them."'

Her voice shook. She bent forward, looking straight at Franklin Clarke.

'I know,' he said. 'I know exactly.'

'Aren't we going to make any plans for the future?' asked Thora Grey.

'Of course,' said Franklin Clarke. 'I think that when the fourth letter comes, we ought to work together.'

'I could make some suggestions,' said Poirot. 'I think it is just possible that the waitress Milly Higley might know something useful. I suggest two ways to find out. You, Miss Barnard, could start an argument with the girl. Say you knew she never liked your sister – and that your sister had told you all about *her*. She will tell you exactly what she thought of your sister.'

'The other way is that Mr Fraser could pretend to be interested in the girl.'

'Is that necessary?' asked Donald Fraser.

'No, it is not necessary. It is just one way to find out more information.'

'Shall *I* try?' asked Franklin Clarke. 'Let me see what I can do with the young lady.'

'You've got your own part of the world to look after,' said Thora Grey rather sharply.

'I don't think there is much you can do down there for the present,' said Poirot. 'Mademoiselle Grey is more suitable for – '

Thora Grey interrupted him.

'But, you see, Monsieur Poirot, I have left Devon now.'

'Miss Grey very kindly stayed to help me organise everything,' said Franklin Clarke. 'But naturally she prefers a job in London.'

Poirot looked from one to the other.

'How is Lady Clarke?' he asked.

I was admiring the pale colour in Thora Grey's face and almost missed Clarke's reply.

'Not good. I wonder if you could come down to Devon and visit her, Monsieur Poirot? She said she would like to see you.'

'Certainly, Mr Clarke. Shall we say the day after tomorrow?'

'Good. I'll tell the nurse.'

'You, my child,' said Poirot, turning to Mary, 'I think you might perhaps do useful work in Andover. Try talking to the children. There were a lot of children playing in the street where your aunt lived. Perhaps they noticed who went in and out of your aunt's shop.'

'Shall I put an advertisement in a newspaper?' asked Clarke. 'Something like this: *A B C. Urgent, H P is close behind you. Give me a hundred pounds for my silence. X Y Z.* It might make him show himself.'

'It is possible to try,' said Poirot. 'But I think that A B C will be too clever to reply.' He smiled. 'Mr Clarke, I think you are like a boy in your heart.'

'Well,' Clarke said, looking at his notebook, 'we're making a start.'

CHAPTER 8

A Sick Lady

'Mad, poor man – the murderer, I mean. I've always been
sorry for mad people – their heads must feel so strange.'

Poirot returned to his seat and sat down.

'It is unfortunate that she is so intelligent,' he said quietly.

'Who?'

'Megan Barnard. Mademoiselle Megan. "Words," she says. She realises that there is no meaning in anything I am saying. Nobody else noticed.'

'Didn't you mean what you said?'

'I simply said the same thing many times.'

'But why?'

'*Eh bien* – to start – shall we say – the conversations. And there is something else, Hastings. Murder can often help people find romance.'

'Poirot!' I cried. I was shocked. 'I'm sure none of these people was thinking of anything except – '

'Did you see how Franklin Clarke suddenly bent forward and looked at Mademoiselle Megan? And did you also notice how annoyed Mademoiselle Thora Grey was about it? And Mr Donald Fraser, he – '

'Poirot,' I said. 'You have a very romantic mind.'

Suddenly the door opened. To my great surprise, Thora Grey entered.

'Forgive me for coming back,' she said. 'But there was something that I think I would like to tell you, Monsieur Poirot.'

'Certainly, mademoiselle. Please sit down.'

Thora Grey sat down and began to speak, choosing her words carefully.

'Mr Clarke told you that I decided to leave Combeside. He is a very kind and loyal person. But it is not quite like that. Lady Clarke wished me to leave. She is very ill, and her brain is confused because of the drugs they give her. The drugs make her suspicious and imaginative. She started to dislike me and told me to leave the house.'

I admired the girl's honesty.

'It's very good of you to come and tell us this,' I said.

'It's always better to be honest,' she said with a little smile. 'It was rather a shock to me,' she said sadly. 'I had no idea Lady Clarke disliked me so much. In fact, I always thought she was rather fond of me.' She got up. 'That's all that I came to say. Goodbye.'

I went downstairs with her.

When I came back, I said, 'I think that was very brave of her.'

'Do you know,' said Poirot, 'I am sure that already, in our conversations this afternoon, something important was said. It is strange – I do not know exactly what it was … *something that reminded me of something which I had already seen or heard or noted …*'

'Something at Churston?'

'No, not at Churston … before that … It doesn't matter. I will remember.'

A few days later we went down to Combeside again to see Lady Clarke. It was a September day at the beginning of autumn. There was a deep sadness surrounding the house. The downstairs rooms were closed. We were shown into a small room where a hospital nurse came to meet us.

'Monsieur Poirot?' she asked. 'I'm Nurse Capstick.'

'How is Lady Clarke?' asked Poirot.

'Not bad. One can't hope for much improvement, of course, but some new treatment has made things a little easier for her.'

'I suppose her husband's death was a terrible shock?' asked Poirot.

'Well, Monsieur Poirot,' said the nurse, 'Lady Clarke doesn't always know what's happening because of the drugs.'

'Were she and her husband very fond of each other?'

'Oh, yes, they were a very happy couple. He was very worried and upset about her, poor man. But he was often busy with his art collection. Miss Grey helped him with that.'

'Oh, yes – Miss Grey. She has left, has she not?'

'Yes – I'm very sorry about it. Sometimes ladies get strange ideas when they're not well.'

She led us upstairs to a room on the first floor. It had been a bedroom but was now a cheerful-looking sitting-room. Lady Clarke was sitting in a big armchair near the window. She was very thin, and her face had the grey look of one who suffers much pain.

'This is Monsieur Poirot, who you wanted to see,' said Nurse Capstick.

'Oh, yes, Monsieur Poirot,' said Lady Clarke, giving him her hand.

'My friend Captain Hastings, Lady Clarke.'

'How do you do? So good of you both to come.'

We sat down. There was a silence.

'It was about Car's death, wasn't it?' said Lady Clarke at last. 'Oh, yes. I told Franklin to ask you to come. I hope Franklin isn't going to be foolish ... Men are so easily fooled ... They are like boys ... especially Franklin.'

'Did you want to say something about your husband's death?' asked Poirot.

'Car's death? Yes, ... Mad, poor man – the murderer, I mean. I've always been sorry for mad people – their heads must feel so strange. You haven't caught him yet?' she asked. 'Surely somebody saw him around here that day.'

'There were so many strangers, Lady Clarke. It is the holiday season.'

'Yes – I forgot ... But they stay down by the beaches.'

'No stranger came to the house that day,' said Poirot.

'Who says so?' asked Lady Clarke in a voice that was surprisingly strong.

'The servants,' said Poirot. 'Miss Grey.'

Lady Clarke said very clearly, 'That girl is a liar!'

I felt shocked. Poirot looked at me quickly.

'I didn't like her. I've never liked her. I sent her away. Franklin said she might be a help to me. Franklin's a fool! I didn't want him getting mixed up with her. "I'll give her three months pay, if you like," I said. "But I don't want her in the house a day longer." There's one good thing about being ill – men can't argue with you. He did what I said and she went.'

'Why did you say that Miss Grey was a liar?' asked Poirot.

'Because she is. She told you that no strangers came to the house. But I saw her, with my own eyes, talking to a strange man on the front doorstep. It was the morning of the day Car died – about eleven o'clock.'

'What did this man look like?'

'An ordinary sort of man. Nothing special.' A look of pain came over her face. 'Please – you must go now – I'm a little tired – '

'That's a very strange story,' I said to Poirot as we travelled back to London. 'About Miss Grey and a strange man.'

'You see, Hastings? *There is always something to be found out.*'

'Why did the girl lie about it and tell us she had seen no one?'

'The easiest way to answer the question is to ask her.'

'It's unbelievable that a girl like her would help a madman.'

'Exactly – so I do not believe it.'

'Lady Clarke doesn't like her because she's good-looking,' I said.

'Perhaps Lady Clarke is right,' said Poirot. 'Perhaps her husband and Franklin Clarke are wrong – and Captain Hastings.' He looked at me in an amused way. 'You always want to help good-looking girls in trouble.'

'How silly you are, Poirot,' I said, laughing.

When we arrived home, we were told that a gentleman was waiting to see Poirot. To my surprise it was Donald Fraser. He seemed very embarrassed and shy. Poirot invited him to have sandwiches and a glass of wine with us.

After we had eaten, Poirot said, 'You have come from Bexhill, Mr Fraser?'

'Yes.' He stopped. 'I don't know why I've come to you!' he said suddenly.

'*I* know,' said Poirot. 'There is something that you must tell someone. You are quite right. I am the correct person. Speak!'

Fraser looked at him gratefully.

'Monsieur Poirot, do you know anything about dreams? I've had the same dream for three nights. I think I'm going mad. I'm on the beach, looking for Betty. She's lost – only lost, you understand. I've got to find her. I've got to give her her belt. I'm carrying it in my hand. And then – '

'Yes?'

'The dream changes ... I'm not looking any more. She's there in front of me – sitting on the beach. She doesn't see me coming. I come up behind her ... she doesn't hear me ... I put the belt round her neck and pull ... She's dead ... I've strangled her – and then her head falls back and I see her face ... and it's *Megan* – not Betty!'

He sat back, white and shaking.

'What's the meaning of it, Monsieur Poirot? Why does it come to me? Every night ... I – I didn't kill her, did I?'

I don't know what Poirot answered, because at that moment I heard the postman's knock. I left the room and went to the letter-box. Then I rushed back into the living-room.

'Poirot,' I cried. 'It's come. The fourth letter.'

He jumped up and took it from me. Then he opened it with his paper-knife. He spread it out on the table. The three of us read it together.

Still no success? What are you and the police doing? Well, well, isn't this fun? Poor Mr Poirot, I'm quite sorry for you.

If at first you don't succeed, try, try again.

We've got a long way to go still.

The next little event will take place at Doncaster on 11 September.

See you.

A B C

Inspector Crome came round from Scotland Yard. While he was still there, Franklin Clarke and Megan Barnard arrived. The girl explained that she, too, had come from Bexhill because she wanted to ask Clarke something. Crome wasn't very pleased to see everyone there. He became very official.

'I'll take this letter with me, Monsieur Poirot,' he said.

'This time we've got to get this man,' said Clarke. 'I should tell you, Inspector, that we've formed our own legion to catch him. I don't think your job is going to be easy. I think A B C has beaten you again.'

'I don't think people will be able to criticise our arrangements this time,' said Crome. 'The fool has given us a lot of warning. The 11th isn't until next Wednesday. We have a lot of time to make this public in the newspapers. We shall warn everyone in Doncaster whose name begins with a D. Also, we'll move a lot of police into the town.'

Clarke said quietly, 'It's easy to see that you're not interested in sport, Inspector.'

Crome stared at him. 'What do you mean, Mr Clarke?'

'Don't you realise that *next Wednesday the St Leger* is being run in Doncaster?*'

The Inspector looked shocked.

'That's true,' he said. 'Yes, that makes things more complicated ...'

We were all silent for a minute or two as we thought about the situation. There would be crowds on the race-course – the sport-loving English public.

'I believe,' said Clarke, 'that the murder will take place on the race-course – perhaps actually while the Leger is being run.'

Inspector Crome got up and left, taking the letter with him.

We heard voices in the hallway. A few minutes later, Thora Grey entered. She went straight to Franklin Clarke and put a hand on his arm. She spoke anxiously, waiting for his answer.

'The Inspector told me there's another letter. Where's the murder going to be this time?'

'Doncaster – and on the day of the St Leger.'

We started discussing the matter. I felt that there was very little hope. What could a small group of six people do?

* the St Leger: a popular horse race that is run every September in Doncaster

5.1 Were you right?

Look at your answers to Activity 4.4. Then complete
Hastings' notes with information about the murder victims.

Name	Place where he/she lived	Job	Relatives/people close to victim
Alice Ascher			
Betty Barnard			
Sir Carmichael Clarke			

5.2 What more did you learn?

Match each thought with one of the people below.

I think he's mad. I'm leaving!

I didn't want to leave Combeside.

I hate that girl!

1 ....

2 ....

3 ....

Why doesn't Poirot *do* something?!

Why do I have this terrible dream?

Inspector Crome is a fool!

6 ....

4 ....

5 ....

a Hastings

b Lady Clarke

c Franklin Clarke

d Thora Grey

e Donald Fraser

f Young man in Princess Gardens

5.3 Language in use

Look at the sentences in the box. Then write *may* or *must* in the spaces below. Inspector Crome is giving advice in a newspaper about the *ABC* murderer.

> 'He **may** be in *your* town!'
>
> 'I've always been sorry for mad people – their heads **must** feel so strange.'

Watch Out for the Mad Killer!

Our reporter interviewed Inspector Crome of Scotland Yard.

'A killer [1].............................. be going round our seaside towns,' said Inspector Crome. 'He always leaves an *ABC* railway guide at the scene of the crime, so he [2].............................. be interested in the railways. And he [3].............................. be very clever because we don't know who he is yet. 'The police are working very hard, and we [4].............................. arrest him at any time now. But he [5].............................. already be planning his next murder. If you see him, do not go near him; he seems to choose his victims carefully, but he [6].............................. be dangerous!'

5.4 What happens next?

1 Look at the picture on page 60.

   a Who is the man in the picture? ....

   b What is he carrying? ....

   c Where do you think he is going? ....

2 Look at the picture on page 61.

   a What has happened? ....

   b What is the young man saying? ....

   c What is the older man saying? ....

3 Look at the words in italics at the top of page 64.

   a Who is being described? ....

   b Why is the knife 'sticky and red'? ....

CHAPTER 9

The Hunt Begins

'You are quite right, mademoiselle,' said Poirot. '"He wasn't the sort of man you'd notice." Yes … You have described the murderer!'

'We know nothing about this man,' said Thora Grey.

'No, no, mademoiselle,' said Poirot. 'That is not true. Each one of us knows something about him. I am sure that the knowledge is there.'

Clarke shook his head.

'We don't know anything. None of us has ever seen him or spoken to him. We've tried to remember everything again and again.'

'Not everything!' said Poirot. 'For example, Miss Grey told us that she did not see or speak to any stranger on the day that Sir Carmichael was killed.'

Thora Grey nodded. 'That's quite right.'

'Is it? *Lady Clarke told us, mademoiselle, that from her window she saw you standing on the front doorstep talking to a man.*'

'She saw *me* talking to a strange man?' The girl seemed very surprised. 'Lady Clarke has made a mistake. I never – Oh! I remember now! How stupid! But it wasn't important. Just one of those men who come round selling stockings. I was crossing the hall when he came to the door.'

Poirot put his hands to his head. Everyone stared at him.

'Stockings,' he said quietly. 'Stockings … it is the connection – three months ago … the other day … and now. *Bon Dieu*, yes!'

He sat up straight and looked at me.

'You remember, Hastings? In the shop at Andover. We went upstairs. On a chair in the bedroom was a pair of new stockings. And you, mademoiselle – ' he turned to Megan, 'you spoke of your mother who cried *because she had bought your sister some new stockings on the day of the murder …*'

He looked round at us all.

'You see? It is the same thing repeated three times. That cannot be coincidence. Remember Mrs Ascher's neighbour, Mrs Fowler. She talked about people who were always trying to *sell* you things – like stockings. Tell me, mademoiselle,' he said to Megan, 'it is true, is it not, that your mother bought those stockings from someone who came to the door?'

'Yes – yes – she did … I remember now.'

'But what's the connection?' cried Franklin Clarke.

'I tell you, my friends, it cannot be coincidence. Three crimes – and each time, a man visits the area selling stockings.'

He turned to Thora. 'Describe this man,' he said.

She looked at him. 'I can't ... I don't know how ... he had glasses, I think – and an old coat ... He wasn't the sort of man you'd notice.'

'You are quite right, mademoiselle,' said Poirot. '*"He wasn't the sort of man you'd notice."* Yes ... You have described the murderer!'

Mr Alexander Bonaparte Cust sat without moving. His breakfast lay cold and untasted on his plate. He was reading a newspaper with great interest.

Suddenly he got up, walked up and down for a minute, then sat down again on a chair by the window. He rested his head in his hands. He didn't hear the sound of the opening door. Mrs Marbury, the owner of the building, stood in the doorway.

'What's the matter, Mr Cust? You haven't touched your breakfast. Is your head hurting you again?'

'No. I mean, yes ... I just feel a little unwell.'

'Well, I'm sorry. You aren't going to go away today, then?'

Mr Cust jumped up quickly.

'No, no, I have to go. It's business. Very important business.' His hands were shaking. 'I'm going to – Cheltenham.'

He said the word so strangely that Mrs Marbury looked at him in surprise.

'Cheltenham's a nice place,' she said conversationally. She bent down and picked up the newspaper, which was lying on the floor.

'The newspapers are full of these murders,' she said. 'Doncaster – that's the place he's going to **carry out** his next murder. And tomorrow! It's the races, too. They say that hundreds of police are being brought in – Mr Cust, you do look bad. Really, you oughtn't to go travelling today.'

'It's necessary, Mrs Marbury. When I've promised to do something, I always do it. It's the only way to succeed in – in – business.'

'But if you're ill?'

'I'm not ill, Mrs Marbury. Just a little worried about – personal matters. I slept badly. I'm really quite all right.'

Mrs Marbury picked up the breakfast things and left the room. Mr Cust took out a suitcase and packed some clothes. Then he unlocked a cupboard. He took out about twelve flat boxes and put them in the suitcase, too.

Lily, Mrs Marbury's daughter, came out of another room.

'Where are you going this time, Mr Cust?,' she said. 'To the seaside again?'

'No, no – er – Cheltenham.'

'Well, that's nice, too. But not quite as nice as Torquay. I want to go there for my holiday next year. You were probably quite near where the murder was – the ABC murder. It happened when you were down there, didn't it?'

'Er – yes. But Churston's ten or eleven kilometres away.'

carry out /ˌkæri ˈaʊt/ (v) to do something that needs to be planned

'How exciting. Perhaps you passed the murderer on the street!'

'Yes, perhaps,' said Mr Cust. He smiled a strange smile.

'Oh, Mr Cust, you *don't* look well,' said Lily.

'I'm quite all right, quite all right. Goodbye, Miss Marbury.'

He picked up his suitcase and hurried out of the front door.

'Funny old thing,' said Lily Marbury to herself. 'He looks half mad.'

Inspector Crome said to his assistant, 'Get me a list of all the companies who make stockings. And I want a list of all their **agents** who go to people's houses selling the stockings.'

'Is this for the ABC case, sir?' asked the assistant.

'Yes. One of Hercule Poirot's ideas.' The Inspector's voice was not very enthusiastic. 'It's probably not important, but we have to check everything.'

'Right, sir, Mr Poirot's done some good work in the past, but I think he's a bit old now, sir.'

'He loves to get attention,' said the Inspector. 'But he's not as clever as he wants people to think. Now, the arrangements for Doncaster ...'

Lily Marbury was dancing with her boyfriend, Tom Hartigan. As they danced, they talked.

'I saw old Mr Cust this morning,' said Tom. 'At Euston Station. He was looking lost, as usual. First he dropped his paper and then he dropped his ticket. I picked it up. He thanked me, but I don't think he recognised me.'

agent /ˈeɪdʒənt/ (n) a person who acts for a company in its business; a **newsagent** owns or manages a shop that sells **newspapers** and other things

'Did you say Euston or Paddington?' asked Lily.

'Euston.'

'That's strange. I thought trains went to Cheltenham from Paddington.'

'That's right. But old Cust wasn't going to Cheltenham. He was going to Doncaster. I saw his ticket.'

'Well, he told *me* he was going to Cheltenham. I'm sure he did.'

'No – you're wrong. He was going to Doncaster.'

'Oh, Tom, I hope he won't get murdered. Doncaster is where the ABC murder is going to happen.'

'Cust will be all right. His name doesn't begin with a D.'

'He was down near Churston at Torquay when the last murder happened.'

'Was he? That's a coincidence, isn't it?' Tom laughed. 'He wasn't at Bexhill before that, was he?'

'He was away ... Yes, I remember he was away,' said Lily, 'because he forgot his swimsuit. Mother was mending it for him.'

'Well, if he wanted his swimsuit, he was at the seaside. Lily,' said Tom with an amused look, 'perhaps old Mr Cust is the murderer!'

'Mr Cust wouldn't hurt anything or anyone,' laughed Lily.

They continued to dance.

Doncaster!

I shall, I think, remember 11 September all my life. We were all there, at the St Leger – Poirot, myself, Clarke, Fraser, Megan Barnard, Thora Grey

and Mary Drower. But *what could any of us do*? Thora Grey was the only person who might be able to recognise the murderer. She wasn't calm and quiet now. She was almost crying, and her hands were shaking.

'I never really looked at him,' she said. 'What a fool I was! Even if I see him again, I might not recognise him. I've got a bad memory for faces.'

Poirot put his hand gently on her shoulder.

'Now, little one, don't be upset,' he said kindly. 'If you see this man, you will recognise him. We have had a lot of bad luck, and our murderer has had a lot of good luck. But now I believe that our luck has changed! The clue of the stockings is the beginning. Now everything will go wrong for him! He, too, will begin to make mistakes ...'

We had agreed that we would walk round as many streets as possible, and later, position ourselves in different parts of the race-course. I had suggested that I should go with one of the ladies, and Poirot had agreed with my idea.

The girls went to put on their hats. Franklin Clarke started to talk to Poirot.

'Listen, Monsieur Poirot. You went down to Churston, I know, and saw my brother's wife. Did she say – I mean, did she suggest – ?'

He stopped, embarrassed. Poirot looked at him with an innocent face.

'Did she suggest – what?'

Franklin Clarke's face was rather red.

'It's about Thora – Miss Grey,' he said. Poirot looked surprised. 'Lady Clarke got certain ideas in her head. You see, Thora – Miss Grey – is rather a good-looking girl – and Lady Clarke became jealous. After Car's death, she got very upset. Of course it's partly the illness and the drugs.

'My brother always said that Miss Grey was the best secretary he ever had – and he was very fond of her, too. But there wasn't any romantic relationship between them. Look,' – he put his hand in his pocket – 'here's a letter I received from my brother when I was in Asia.'

You may remember Thora Grey? She is a dear girl and a great help to me. She loves beautiful things and shares my enthusiasm for Chinese art. I was very lucky to find her. No daughter could be closer to me.'

'You see,' said Franklin. 'My brother thought of her like a daughter. I wanted to show you this, because I didn't want you to get the wrong idea about Thora from anything that Lady Clarke said.'

Poirot returned the letter.

'You can be sure,' he said, smiling, 'that I never allow myself to get the wrong idea from anything that anyone tells me. I form my own judgements.'

The girls came back and we left the room. Then Poirot called me back.

'Which lady do you intend to go with, Hastings?' he asked.

'Well – I – er – I hadn't thought about it yet.'

'What about Miss Barnard?'

'She's rather an independent type,' I said.

'Miss Grey?'

'Yes. She's better.'

'Hastings, you are not being honest with me,' said Poirot. 'All the time you wanted to spend the day with Miss Grey!'

'Oh, Poirot!' I said.

'I am sorry to upset your plans,' said Poirot, 'but I request you to go with Mary Drower – and I must ask that you do not leave her.'

'But, Poirot, why?'

'Because, my dear friend, her name begins with a D. We must be very careful.'

I realised that Poirot was right. If A B C hated Poirot, he might be watching his movements. He might kill Mary Drower to show Poirot that he was cleverer than my friend.

I promised to do as Poirot asked.

CHAPTER 10

Death at the Cinema

He put his hand in his pocket and brought out something –
a long thin knife … that was sticky and red …

Mr Leadbetter was at the Regal Cinema in Doncaster. At the most exciting part of the film, the man next to him got up and pushed past him. Then he dropped his hat over the seat in front and bent over to get it back. Mr Leadbetter was very annoyed. He had looked forward to seeing this film for a whole week. Why couldn't people wait until the end of a film?

The annoying gentleman went out. Mr Leadbetter watched the film happily until the end. When the lights went up, he got up slowly. He never left the cinema very quickly.

He looked around. There weren't many people this afternoon – naturally. It was the day of the St Leger and they were all at the races. Everyone was hurrying towards the exit. Mr Leadbetter started to follow. The man in the seat in front of him was asleep.

'Excuse *me*, sir,' said a man who was trying to get past the sleeping gentleman.

Mr Leadbetter reached the exit. He looked back. Something seemed to be happening … perhaps the man in front of him was drunk and not asleep … He stopped for a moment, and then went out.

The manager was saying to the man who had tried to get past, 'He's ill … ' He spoke to the sleeping man. 'What's the matter, sir?'

The other man touched the sleeper. He took his hand away, and looked at a red sticky mark.

'Blood …'

The manager saw the corner of something under the seat.

'It's an – ABC,' he said.

Mr Cust left the Regal Cinema and looked up at the sky. It was a beautiful evening ... a really beautiful evening ...

He walked along smiling to himself until he came to the Black Horse, where he was staying. He climbed the stairs to his bedroom, a small room on the second floor. As he entered the room, he suddenly stopped smiling. There was a mark on the arm of his coat. He touched it – wet and red – blood ...

He put his hand in his pocket and brought out something – a long thin knife ... that was sticky and red ...

Mr Cust sat down and looked around the room like a hunted animal.

'It isn't my fault,' he said. He passed his tongue over his lips. Then he went over to the sink and filled it with water. He took off his coat and washed the arm. The water was red now ...

There was a knock on the door. He stood there, frozen with fear. The door opened. It was a young woman carrying some water.

'Oh, excuse me, sir. Your hot water, sir.'

'Thank you ... I've washed in cold water ...' Immediately she looked at the water in the sink. 'I – I've cut my hand ...' said Mr Cust quickly.

There was a pause – yes, surely a very long pause – before she said, 'Yes, sir.'

She went out, shutting the door. Mr Cust stood and listened. Were there voices – feet coming up the stairs? He could hear only the beating of his own heart. Then suddenly he moved. He put on his coat, went to the door and opened it. There was no one outside. He went quietly down the stairs.

He ran out of the door that opened onto the hotel car park. A couple of drivers were there, talking about the races. Mr Cust hurried across the car park and out into the street. Should he go to the station? Yes – there would be crowds there – special trains. With a bit of luck, he could get away.

Inspector Crome was interviewing Mr Leadbetter. The Chief Constable, **Colonel** Anderson, was there, too.

'Please tell me everything clearly,' said Crome. 'This man went out towards the end of the main film? As he passed you, he fell – '

'He *pretended* to fall. I understand it now. He bent over the seat in front to pick up his hat. He surely **stabbed** the man then. Then he went out.'

'Can you describe him?'

'He was a very big man.'

'Fair or dark?'

Colonel /ˈkɜːnl/ (n) an officer who has or had an important position in the army
stab /stæb/ (v) to push a knife into someone

'I – well, I'm not exactly sure. He was an ugly-looking man.'

Inspector Crome nodded. Then he interviewed the cinema manager. The manager told Crome about the blood on the dead man's coat and the *ABC* railway guide under the seat.

'Did you notice a man leaving the cinema a few minutes earlier?'

'There were several, sir.'

Just then a police constable came in.

'Mr Hercule Poirot's here, sir, and another gentleman.'

Inspector Crome didn't look pleased.

'Oh, well,' he said. 'They'd better come in, I suppose.'

Poirot and I entered the room. Both Crome and Colonel Anderson were looking worried. Colonel Anderson greeted us with a nod of the head.

'I'm glad you've come, Monsieur Poirot,' he said politely.

'Another ABC murder?'

'Yes. The murderer bent over and stabbed the victim in the back. There was an *ABC* on the floor between the dead man's feet.'

'Do you know who the dead man is?' asked Poirot.

'Yes, I think A B C's made a mistake this time. The dead man is called Earlsfield – George Earlsfield. He missed out the letter D.'

My friend shook his head doubtfully.

'Shall we talk to the man who found him?' asked Crome. 'He's anxious to get home.'

A middle-aged gentleman came in. He spoke in an excited, high voice.

'It's the most shocking experience I've ever known,' he said.

'Your name, please,' said the Inspector.

'Downes. Roger Emmanuel Downes. I'm a teacher at a boys' school.'

'Now, Mr Downes, please tell us in your own words what happened.'

'At the end of the film I got up from my seat. The seat on my left was empty but in the seat next to that there was a man who seemed to be asleep. I realised that he was ill, and I called out, "Fetch the manager." As I couldn't pass him, I put my hand on his shoulder to wake him. Then I took my hand from the man's shoulder. I found that it was wet and red ...'

Colonel Anderson was looking at Mr Downes.

'Mr Downes, you're a very lucky man. You're about the same height as the dead man. I think the murderer became confused. He followed you into the cinema but *he chose the wrong victim.* I am sure, Mr Downes, that that knife was meant for you!'

Mr Downes became weak with shock. He sat down on a chair.

'You mean that this madman has followed me? But why me?'

He got up. He suddenly looked old and shaken. 'If you don't want me anymore, gentlemen, I think I'll go home. I – I don't feel very well.'

Mr Downes left the room.

'Send a couple of constables to watch his house,' said Colonel Anderson.

'You think,' said Poirot, 'that when A B C finds out his mistake, he might try to murder Mr Downes again?'

Anderson nodded. 'It's a possibility,' he said. 'A B C may be upset if things don't go according to his plans.'

A constable came in.

'Mr Ball of the Black Horse is here with a young woman, sir,' he said. 'He thinks he has something to tell you which may be helpful.'

Mr Ball was a large, slow-thinking, heavily-moving man. He smelled strongly of beer. With him there was a young woman with round eyes. She seemed to be very excited.

'This girl, Mary, has something to tell you,' said Mr Ball.

Mary told us that she had taken hot water to one of the hotel guests in his room. He was washing his hands. He had taken his coat off and was holding the arm of it in the water in the sink. The coat was wet and the water in the sink was red.

'Red?' said Anderson sharply. 'When was this?'

'At about a quarter to five.'

'More than three hours ago,' said Anderson. 'Why didn't you come at once?'

'We didn't know that there'd been another murder,' said Ball. 'When we heard the news, Mary screamed out about the blood in the sink. I went upstairs to the room, but there was nobody there. One of the men in the car park said he saw a man leaving. So I told Mary to come to the police.'

'Describe this man,' said Inspector Crome to Mary.

'He wasn't very tall or short,' said Mary. 'And he stooped and wore glasses. He was wearing a dark suit and a hat. His clothes looked old and cheap.'

Inspector Crome sent two men to the Black Horse. They came back about ten minutes later and brought the hotel book, which all guests had to sign. We crowded around it. There was a signature there in small writing.

'A B Case – or is it Cash?' said Colonel Anderson.

'A B C,' said Crome.

'What about his luggage?' asked Anderson.

'We found a suitcase in his room, sir, full of small boxes.'

'What was in them?'

'Stockings, sir.'

'Congratulations,' Crome said to Poirot. 'Your guess was right.'

Inspector Crome was in his office at Scotland Yard. The telephone on his desk rang. It was one of the policemen who was helping him on the case.

'Jacobs speaking, sir. A man has come with a story that you ought to hear.'

A few minutes later there was a knock on the door. Jacobs appeared with a tall young man.

'This is Mr Tom Hartigan, sir. He's got something to tell us which may be important in the ABC case.'

The Inspector got up and shook hands with the visitor.

'Good morning, Mr Hartigan. Sit down. What do you want to tell me?'

'Well,' began Tom nervously, 'I've got a young lady friend, you see, and her mother rents out rooms in her house. One of the rooms has been rented for over two years to a man called Cust.'

Tom told the Inspector about his meeting with Mr Cust at Euston Station, and the ticket for Doncaster which Mr Cust had dropped.

'Lily – my young lady – also told me that Mr Cust was near Churston at the time of the murder, and at the seaside when the Bexhill murder happened.

'The newspapers said that information was wanted about A B Case or Cash. Lily's mother, Mrs Marbury, told me that Mr Cust is A B Cust. Then we wondered if Mr Cust had been away from home on the date of the Andover murder. And we remembered that he was.'

Inspector Crome listened to everything carefully. 'You were quite right to come here,' he said. 'These dates may be only a coincidence, and the name, too. But I'd certainly like to interview Mr Cust. Is he at home now?'

'Yes, sir.'

'When did he return?'

'On the evening of the Doncaster murder, sir. He's stayed in a lot since then. And he doesn't look very well, Mrs Marbury says. He buys a lot of newspapers. Mrs Marbury says that he talks to himself, too.'

Tom gave Inspector Crome Mrs Marbury's address.

'Thank you,' said the Inspector. 'I shall probably visit the house later today. Please be careful if you meet Mr Cust. Good morning, Mr Hartigan.'

Tom went outside. Lily Marbury was waiting for him. He told her about his meeting with Inspector Crome.

'The police are going to come and ask him some questions,' he said.

'Poor Mr Cust,' said Lily.

'Don't feel sorry for him. If he's A B C, he's murdered four people.'

Lily shook her head. 'It does seem awful,' she said.

'Come and have some lunch,' said Tom.

'All right. But I must just telephone someone. A girl I was going to meet.'

She ran across the road and came back, looking rather red in the face. She put her arm through Tom's arm.

'Tell me more about Scotland Yard. You didn't see the other man there? The Belgian gentleman. The one that A B C writes to.'

'No. He wasn't there.'

'Well, tell me all about it. Who did you speak to and what did you say?'

Mr Cust put the phone back very gently. He turned to where Mrs Marbury was standing watching him.

'You don't often have a telephone call, Mr Cust,' she said. 'I hope it's not bad news?'

'No – no.' He saw that Mrs Marbury was holding a newspaper. He read *Births – Marriages – Deaths …*

'My sister's just had a little boy,' he said quickly.

'Well, that is nice,' said Mrs Marbury. She wondered why Mr Cust had never said he had a sister. 'Well, Mr Cust, my congratulations. Is it the first one, or have you other little nephews and nieces?'

'It's the only one,' said Mr Cust. 'The only one I've ever had or am likely to have and – er – I think I must go there at once. They – they want me to come. I – I think I can just catch a train if I hurry.'

'Will you be away long, Mr Cust?' called Mrs Marbury, as he ran up the stairs.

'Oh, no – two or three days, that's all.'

He disappeared into his bedroom. A few minutes later, he came quietly down the stairs carrying a bag in his hand. He saw the telephone and remembered the short conversation he had just had.

'Is that you, Mr Cust? I thought you might like to know that an inspector from Scotland Yard may come to see you ... '

Why had Lily telephoned him? Had she guessed his secret? How did she know that the Inspector was coming? Did she *know* ... But surely if she knew, she wouldn't ... Women were very strange, surprisingly cruel and surprisingly kind. Lily was a kind girl. A kind, pretty girl.

He paused in the hall. Then he heard a noise from the kitchen.

Mrs Marbury might come out ...

He opened the front door, passed through it and closed it behind him.

Where ...?

Poirot and I were having another meeting with the Chief Constable, Colonel Anderson and Inspector Crome.

'I've got a list of people in the Churston area where the man went and offered stockings,' said Inspector Crome. 'He stayed at a small hotel. He returned there at 10.30 on the night of the murder.

'He did the same thing in Bexhill. He stayed at a hotel under his own name, and offered stockings to people at about twelve addresses, including Mrs Barnard and including the Orange Cat. He did the same in Andover. He stayed at a small hotel there, too, and offered stockings to Mrs Fowler, next door to Mrs Ascher, and to several other people in the same street.

'I went to the address which Mr Hartigan gave me,' said the Inspector, 'but I found that Cust had left the house about half an hour before. He received a telephone message. Mrs Marbury said it was the first time.

'I searched his room very carefully. I found notepaper there similar to the paper which the letters were written on. There was also a large quantity of stockings – and at the back of the same cupboard there were *eight new ABC railway guides!*'

'That proves he's guilty,' said Colonel Anderson.

'I've found something else, too,' said the Inspector. 'I only found it this morning, sir. There was no sign of the knife in his room, but I thought perhaps he'd brought it back to the house and hidden it somewhere. I found it immediately. The coatstand – no one ever moves a coatstand. I moved it away from the wall – and there it was! The knife! The dried blood was still on it.'

'Good work, Crome,' said Colonel Anderson. 'We only need one thing more now. The man himself.'

'Don't worry, we'll get him,' said Crome.

'But there is something that worries me very much,' said Poirot. 'It is the *why*? The *motive*.'

'But, my dear Poirot, the man's crazy,' said Colonel Anderson impatiently. 'Well, as you say, Crome, it's just a matter of time before we find him.'

Mr Cust stood by a fruit and vegetable shop, staring across the road. Yes, that was it. *A. Ascher. Newsagent.* In the empty window there was a sign: 'Shop to Rent.'

He walked slowly back towards the main street of the town. It was difficult – very difficult – now that he hadn't any more money ... He hadn't had anything to eat all day.

He looked at a board outside another newsagent's shop.

THE ABC CASE. MURDERER STILL FREE. Interviews with Hercule Poirot.

Mr Cust said to himself, 'Hercule Poirot. I wonder if he knows.'

He continued walking. Where was he going? He didn't know. He had come to the end.

He looked up. There were lights in front of him. And letters ...

Police Station.

'That's funny,' said Mr Cust. He gave a little laugh.

Then he stepped inside. Suddenly, as he did so, he fell forward.

6.1 Were you right?

1 Look at your answers to Activity 5.4. Then discuss these questions.

   a What do you know about Mr Alexander Bonaparte Cust?

   b Do you think he is the murderer? Why (not)?

   c Was Lily Marbury right to telephone Mr Cust? Why (not)?

2 Discuss why these are important in the story.

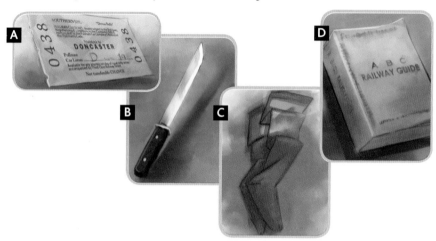

6.2 What more did you learn?

Whose words or thoughts are these? Who are they about?

1 'I never really looked at him. What a fool I was!'

....

2 'But he's not as clever as he wants people to think.'

....

3 'I was very lucky to find her. No daughter could be closer to me.'

....

4 Had she guessed his secret? How did she know that the inspector was coming?

....

5 'I wonder if *he* knows.'

....

6.3 Language in use

Look at the sentence in the box. Then find the endings of the sentences below.

> He **had taken** his coat off and was holding the arm of it in the water in the sink.

1	Mr Cust had bought a ticket and ...	was looking for her employer.
2	Mr Leadbetter had found a good seat and ...	was hurrying to catch the train.
3	Mr Cust had packed his suitcase and ...	was dancing with Tom.
4	Lily had drunk her tea and ...	were making plans.
5	The Special Legion had met in Doncaster and ...	was going downstairs.
6	Mary had seen the blood in the sink and ...	was enjoying the film.

6.4 What happens next?

1 **Look at the picture on page 79.**

    a Where are Poirot and Mr Cust? ....

    b Why is Poirot there? ....

    c What is going to happen to Mr Cust? ....

2 **Work with another student and act out a possible conversation between Poirot and Mr Cust.**

3 **Think again about your answers to Activity 6.1. Is the case finished, do you think? Complete the sentences in the box.**

WHO IS THE MURDERER?

    a Is it Mr Cust? YES/NO

    ....

    b If it is, what is his motive? ....

    ....

    ....

    c If not, who is ABC? ....

    ....

    ....

CHAPTER 11

And Catch a Fox

*'He said the whole country would talk about me.
But he said – he said – I would die a violent death.'*

It was a clear November day. Dr Thompson and Chief Inspector Japp had come to tell Poirot about the police case against Alexander Bonaparte Cust.

'What's your opinion of Cust?' Poirot asked Dr Thompson.

'I don't know. He doesn't seem to be mad. He's an **epileptic**, of course.'

'Yes, that was clear when he fell into the police station in Andover,' I said. 'But can a man murder someone and not know they've done it?'

'In my opinion Cust knows very well that he's responsible for murder,' said Dr Thompson. 'The letters prove that the murders were planned crimes.'

'And we still have no explanation for the letters,' said Poirot. 'Until I know why they were written, I shall not feel that the case is solved.'

'Well, I must go,' said Dr Thompson.

He went out. Japp stayed.

'So Cust has an **alibi** for the Bexhill murder,' said Poirot.

'Yes,' said the Inspector. 'And his alibi is very strong. A man called Strange has told us that he met Cust in the Whitecross Hotel in Eastbourne on the evening of 24 July.

'After dinner he and Cust played cards. Cust played very well. They played cards until midnight, and separated at ten minutes past midnight. So if Cust was in a hotel in Eastbourne at that time, he couldn't strangle Betty Barnard on the beach at Bexhill between midnight and one o'clock. Eastbourne is about twenty-two kilometres away from Bexhill and it would take some time for him to get there.'

'It is a problem – yes,' said Poirot.

'We know that Cust carried out the Doncaster murder – the coat with the blood, the knife – that's certain. He carried out the Churston murder. He carried out the Andover murder. So he also did the Bexhill murder. But I don't understand how!'

'Tell me, Hastings,' said Poirot, after Japp had gone. 'Do you think the case is finished?'

'Well – yes. We've got the man. And we've got most of the facts.'

Poirot shook his head.

---

epileptic /ˌepɪˈleptɪk/ (n) someone who suffers from **epilepsy**, a medical condition affecting the brain that can make them unable to control their movements

alibi /ˈælɪbaɪ/ (n) information that proves that a person was not responsible for a crime because he or she was in another place at that time

'But until we know all about the man, the mystery is as deep as ever. And we know nothing at all! We know where he was born. We know that he fought in the war and was hit on the head. We know that he left the army because he is an epileptic. We know that he rented a room from Mrs Marbury. We know that he is very quiet and shy – the kind of man that nobody notices.

'We know that he planned and carried out several very clever murders. We know that he made some stupid mistakes. We know that he killed without pity. We know that he did not want anyone else to suffer for his crimes. Do you not see, Hastings, that the man is like two different people?

'All the time I have tried *to get to know the murderer.* And now I realise, Hastings, *that I do not know him at all!* I am quite confused. *Why* did he carry out these murders? *Why* did he choose those people?'

'Alphabetically – ' I began.

'Was Betty Barnard the only person in Bexhill whose name began with a B? Betty Barnard – I had an idea there ... It ought to be true – it must be true. But if it is – '

He was silent for some time. I didn't like to interrupt him, and I believe I fell asleep. Suddenly I woke to find Poirot's hand on my shoulder.

'*Mon cher* Hastings,*' he said. 'Always you help me – you bring me luck.'

I was quite confused. 'How have I helped you this time?' I asked.

'I remembered something that you said. It makes everything very clear. I see the answers to all my questions. The reason for Mrs Ascher, the reason for Sir Carmichael Clarke, the reason for the Doncaster murder, and finally – very important – *the reason for Hercule Poirot.*

'But first, I need a little more information from our Special Legion. And then – then, *when I have got an answer to one of my questions, I will go and see A B C.* We will face each other at last – A B C and Hercule Poirot – the enemies. And then – we will talk!'

'What do you expect Cust to tell you?' I asked.

Hercule Poirot smiled.

'A lie,' he said. 'And from the lie, I shall know the truth!'

During the next few days, Poirot was very busy. He was mysteriously absent for a lot of the time. He talked very little and refused to answer any of my questions. But towards the end of the week, he said he intended to visit Bexhill. He suggested that I should come with him and I agreed enthusiastically. The members of our Special Legion were also invited.

Poirot first visited Mr and Mrs Barnard and asked them when exactly Cust had come to their door, and what he had said. Then he went to the hotel where Cust

* *mon cher*: French for 'my dear'

had stayed and asked for a detailed description of Cust. Next, he went to the beach – to the place where Betty Barnard's body had been discovered. He studied the ground carefully.

He then walked from the beach to the nearest place where a car could be parked. From there he went to the place where the Eastbourne buses waited before leaving Bexhill.

Finally he took us all to the Orange Cat café, where the fat waitress, Milly Higley, served us tea.

'I have finished in Bexhill,' said Poirot. 'I will go to Eastbourne. I need to ask one question there. It is not necessary for you all to come with me. But come back to the hotel and let us have a drink. That tea was horrible!'

As we were having our drinks, Franklin Clarke said, 'I suppose we can guess what you're trying to do. You're trying to prove that Cust's alibi is false. You seem very pleased, but I don't know why. You haven't got a new fact of any kind.'

'No – that is true,' said Poirot. Then he continued, 'My friend Hastings told me once that he had, as a young man, played a game called The Truth. Everyone was asked three questions. They had to promise to answer two questions truthfully.' He paused. '*Eh bien*, I want to play that game. But one will be enough. One question to each of you.'

'Of course,' said Clarke impatiently. 'We'll answer anything.'

'Ah, but I want it to be more serious than that. Do you all promise to speak the truth?'

Everyone became as serious as Poirot. They all promised. Then Poirot turned to Franklin Clarke.

'What did you think of the hats that the ladies wore at Ascot* this year?'

Franklin Clarke stared at him in surprise.

'Is this a joke?'

'Certainly not.'

Clarke began to smile. 'Well, Monsieur Poirot, I didn't actually go to Ascot, but I saw some of the women driving to the races and their hats this year were an even bigger joke than the hats they usually wear.'

Poirot smiled and turned to Donald Fraser.

'When did you take your holiday this year?'

Fraser stared. 'My holiday? The first two weeks in August.'

Then Poirot turned to Thora Grey and I heard a slight change in his voice. His question came sharp and clear.

'Mademoiselle, after Lady Clarke's death, did you hope to marry Sir Carmichael?'

---

* Ascot: a famous yearly race meeting where ladies wear fashionable hats

76

The girl jumped up. 'How dare you ask me such a question! It's insulting!'

'Perhaps. But you have promised to speak the truth. Yes or no?'

'Sir Carmichael was wonderfully kind to me. He treated me almost like a daughter. And that's how I felt to him – I was fond of him, and grateful, too.'

'Excuse me, but that is not answering yes or no, mademoiselle.'

'The answer, of course, is no!'

He turned to Megan Barnard. The girl's face was very pale.

'Mademoiselle, what do you hope will be the result of my questions? Do you want me to find out the truth or not?'

Megan's head went back proudly. 'No!' she said clearly.

We all jumped. Poirot sat forward, studying her face.

'Mademoiselle Megan,' he said, 'you may not want the truth but – you can speak it!' he said.

He turned towards the door, then remembered Mary Drower.

'Tell me, have you a young man?'

Mary looked at him nervously. 'Oh, Mr Poirot. I – I – well, I'm not sure.'

Poirot smiled. Then he looked round for me.

'Come, Hastings, we must start for Eastbourne.'

The car was waiting and soon we were driving along the coast road that leads through Pevensey to Eastbourne. Poirot seemed very pleased with himself. As we passed through Pevensey, he suggested that we should stop and look at the castle there. As we were returning to the car, we passed a group of children in a circle singing a song.

'What is it that they are saying, Hastings?' asked Poirot.

I listened until I understood.

'*– And catch a* **fox**
And put him in a box
And never let him go.'

Poirot repeated the words. His face suddenly became very serious.

'That is very terrible, Hastings.' He was silent. 'You hunt the fox here?'

'*I* don't. I've never been able to afford to hunt. And I don't think there's much hunting in this part of the world.'

'I meant in England generally. A strange sport. The dogs run after the fox and at last they catch him and he dies – quickly and horribly. But the quick, cruel death is better than what those children were singing ... It is not good to be shut away – in a box – for ever ... Tomorrow, I am going to visit Cust. Now let's go back to London.'

'Aren't we going to Eastbourne?' I cried.

'What for? I know quite enough now.'

♦

I was not present at the interview between Poirot and that strange man, Alexander Bonaparte Cust. Because of his relationship with the police, Poirot was able to be there, but I wasn't included in the special permission that was needed. Poirot also wanted the interview to be completely private – the two men face to face. But when Poirot came back, he told me all about it in great detail.

Mr Cust seemed smaller, and to stoop even more. His fingers pulled nervously at his coat. For a time, Poirot sat and looked at him.

At last he said gently, 'Do you know who I am?'

Mr Cust shook his head. 'No – no, I don't. Or are you from Mr Maynard – from his law office?' He was polite, but didn't seem very interested. His mind seemed to be on something else, something inside himself.

'I am Hercule Poirot ...'

He said the words very gently ... and watched for the effect. Mr Cust lifted his head a little.

'Oh yes?' he said. Then, a minute later, he repeated the words again. 'Oh yes?' This time he sounded different – more interested. He looked at Poirot.

Poirot looked back and nodded.

'Yes,' he said. 'I am the man that you wrote the letters to.'

At once, the contact was broken. Mr Cust dropped his eyes and spoke crossly.

'I never wrote to you,' he said. 'Those letters weren't written by me. I've said so again and again.'

fox /fɒks/ (n) a wild animal like a dog, red-brown in colour with a thick tail

'I know,' said Poirot. 'But if you did not write them, who did?'

'An enemy. I must have an enemy. They are all against me. The police – everyone – all against me.'

Poirot didn't reply.

'Everyone has been against me – always.'

'Even when you were a child?'

Mr Cust seemed to think about that.

'No – no – not exactly then. My mother was very fond of me. She thought I was going to be special – that I could do anything.'

He was silent for a minute.

'But she was quite wrong. I was afraid of people. I had a bad time at school. And later, when I started work, I had the feeling that everyone thought I was stupid.'

'And in the war?' asked Poirot.

'You know,' said Mr Cust, and his face lit up, 'I enjoyed the war. I felt, for the first time, like a man.' His smile disappeared. 'But then I got hit on the head, so they made me leave the army. I started working in an office, but things were very difficult. I had very little money. And then I got the offer of the job selling stockings.'

'You told us the name of the company. But you know now, don't you,' said Poirot in a gentle voice, 'that that company didn't employ you?'

'That's because they're against me too. I've got their letters to me, giving me instructions about places to go to, and a list of people to visit.'

'Their letters weren't written,' said Poirot. 'They were typed. All those letters were typed on the machine which was found in your room. So it seems that *you typed them yourself and posted them to yourself?*'

'No, no!' said Mr Cust. 'It's because they're all against me.'

'And the *ABCs* that were found in the cupboard?'

'I know nothing about them. I thought they were stockings.'

'Why did you put a mark by the name of Mrs Ascher in that first list of people in Andover?'

'Because I decided to visit her first. One must begin somewhere. But I didn't murder her! I'm completely innocent. It's all a mistake. Look at that second crime – the Bexhill one. I was playing cards in Eastbourne.'

'You play cards very well, I believe,' said Poirot.

'I – I, well, I believe I do. You'd be surprised how a game of cards can bring strangers together. I remember one man – I've never forgotten him because of something he told me. We just got talking over a cup of coffee, and we started playing cards.'

'What did he tell you?' asked Poirot.

Mr Cust's face looked worried.

'He read my future in my hand. He said I would be one of the most famous men in England before I died. He said the whole country would talk about me. But he said – he said – I would die a violent death.' He was silent suddenly. 'My head … I suffer very badly … I get cruel headaches sometimes. And then there are times when I don't know …'

He stopped.

'But you do know, don't you,' Poirot said, *'that you carried out the murders!'*

Mr Cust looked up. He looked strangely at peace.

'Yes,' he said. 'I know.'

'But – I am right, am I not? – *you don't know why you carried them out?*'

Mr Cust shook his head.

'No,' he said. 'I don't.'

CHAPTER 12

Poirot Explains

'You must realise that you are a very famous man.
Probably the most famous man in England.'

Poirot called a meeting of the Special Legion.
'From the beginning,' he said, 'I have been worried about the why of this case. The mystery was *not the mystery of the murders, but the mystery of A B C.* Why was it necessary for him to carry out these murders? Why did he choose me as his enemy?

'It is no answer to say that the man was mad. As soon as I received the first letter, I was upset and worried. It seemed to me that there was something very wrong about the letter.'

'You were quite right,' said Franklin Clarke.

'Yes. But then, at the beginning, I made a serious mistake. The letter made me very worried. The police thought it was a joke. I was sure that a murder would happen in Andover. As you know, a murder *did* happen.

'There was no way of knowing who the person was who had carried out the murder. I had to try and understand what *kind* of a person had done it. I had to discover the motive of the crime, the motive of the letter.

'Why did the murderer send the letter to *me*? Why not to Scotland Yard, or to a newspaper? Why to Hercule Poirot? Was it for a *personal reason*?

'Then the second letter arrived – and was followed by the murder of Betty Barnard. It became clear now that the murders were going to take place according to an alphabetical plan. But *why* did A B C need to carry out these murders?

'When we think about the four victims – or three of them (since I know very little about Mr Downes or Mr Earlsfield) – we realise that it was possible for the murderer to kill them without anyone suspecting him. The clear suspects were Franz Ascher, Donald Fraser or Megan Barnard, or possibly Mr Clarke. Why, then, did the murderer need to call attention to himself? Why did he need to leave on each body an *ABC* railway guide?

'I was learning certain things about the murderer. His crimes were listed alphabetically – that was clearly important. His victims were men and women, and of different ages. So age and sex were not important to him.

'The choice of the *ABC* suggested to me that it was someone who was interested in railways. This is more common in men than in women. Small boys love trains more than small girls. It might be a sign, too, of someone whose mind was not of an adult – someone who was still a "boy".

'The death of Betty Barnard gave me other clues. She was strangled with her own belt – therefore she was killed by someone she was friendly with. Betty Barnard liked attention from good-looking men. She went out with A B C, so he was attractive to women.'

Donald Fraser jumped up angrily.

'Mr Poirot – please.'

'It is finished,' said Poirot. 'I will say no more. We will pass to the next murder, the murder of Sir Carmichael Clarke. Here the murderer goes back to his first method – hitting the victim on the head. We were unlucky over this crime since the warning letter did not reach us in time. Therefore no preparations could be made to stop the crime.

'Then the clue of the stockings was discovered. The appearance of a stocking-seller near the scene of each crime could not be a coincidence. So he must be the murderer. But his description, as given by Miss Grey, did not match my picture of the man who strangled Miss Barnard.

'A fourth murder was carried out – the murder of a man named George Earlsfield – in mistake, we thought, for a man named Downes. And now the murderer's luck changes and A B C is at last arrested. The case, as Hastings says, has ended! The man is in prison. Finish!

'*But not for me!* I still don't know the *why*! And there is one small annoying fact. The man Cust has an alibi for the night of the Bexhill crime.'

'That's been worrying me, too,' said Franklin Clarke.

'Yes,' continued Poirot. 'The alibi seems real. But it cannot be real unless ... and now we come to two very interesting ideas. Supposing, my friends, that while Cust was responsible for three of the crimes – the A, C and D crimes – *he did not carry out the B crime.*'

'Monsieur Poirot. It isn't – ' said Megan Barnard.

Poirot silenced Megan Barnard with a look.

'Be quiet, mademoiselle,' said Poirot. 'I want the truth! I have finished with lies. Suppose, I say, that someone else murdered Betty Barnard.'

'Monsieur Poirot! Surely all the crimes were done by the same person!'

Poirot took no notice of Megan and continued, 'I told you that there was a second idea. Supposing that someone else killed Betty Barnard? Did that someone else do the other murders, too?'

'But that doesn't make sense!' cried Clarke.

'Doesn't it? I examined the letters again. I had felt from the beginning that there was something wrong with them. I had thought they were written by a madman. But then I realised – they were not. They were false. The writer was only *pretending* to be mad.

'What would be the reason for writing such letters? To call the police's attention to the murders! At first, it did not seem to make sense. And then I saw light. It was to call the police's attention to *several* murders – to a *group* of murders, so that one of those murders would not be noticed!

'I was facing a very clever murderer. *Not* Mr Cust! I was facing a very different kind of man – a man who enjoyed behaving like a boy (remember the schoolboy-like letters and the railway guide) and who was attractive to women. A man who played an important part in one of the crimes!

'I thought about all the crimes again. The Andover crime? The most likely suspect was Franz Ascher, but I could not imagine that Ascher could invent and carry out such a complicated plan. The Bexhill crime? Donald Fraser was clever and had ability, but his motive for killing his girlfriend could only be jealousy. It was very unlikely that such a crime would be planned.

'We now come to the Churston crime. Sir Carmichael Clarke was a very rich man. Who will get his money after he dies? His wife, who is dying, and then it goes to *his brother, Franklin.*'

Poirot turned slowly round and looked at Franklin Clarke.

'I was quite sure then. *A B C and Franklin Clarke were the same person!* Franklin Clarke is attractive to women – he could easily make a girl in a café go out with him. He enjoys making lists – he made a list here one day. And finally, his boyish behaviour – Lady Clarke told us about that. I was quite sure in my own mind. The writer of the letters and the murderer was *Franklin Clarke.*'

Franklin Clarke started to laugh.

'And what about our friend Cust? What about the blood on his coat? And the knife he hid? He may say he didn't do the crimes – '

'You are quite wrong,' said Poirot. 'He says he *did* do the murders. He believes himself to be guilty. But as soon as I saw him, I knew he could not be guilty. He is not clever enough. No, there were two people who played a part in these crimes. The real murderer – clever and daring – and the false murderer – weak and stupid.

'I think you had the idea when you first met Mr Cust in a coffee shop. You were thinking about murdering your brother. You showed me a letter your brother had written to you. In it he showed how fond he was of Miss Thora Grey. You were afraid that when Lady Clarke died, your brother might marry Miss Grey and have children. Then you would not get any of his money.

'Your meeting with Mr Cust gave you an idea. His strange names, his epilepsy and his weak character made him the tool that you were looking for. The whole alphabetical plan jumped into your mind.

'You contacted a company that made stockings and asked for a large number of stockings to be sent to Cust. You sent him a number of *ABC* railway guides. You wrote a letter to him, pretending that it came from the stocking company and offering him good pay for selling stockings. You made your plans so well that you typed all the letters that were sent later. *Then you gave him the machine on which they were typed.*

'You found two victims whose names began with A and B. You sent a list of customers in the Andover area to Cust, telling him to go there on a certain date. Mrs Ascher's name was on the list. You sent the first A B C letter to me. Then you went to Andover and killed Mrs Ascher. For the second murder, you probably killed Betty Barnard before midnight on the 24th.

'We now come to murder number 3 – the important murder for you. And here I must thank Hastings. *He suggested that the third letter was sent to the wrong address on purpose.* And he was right …

'I had wondered … why were the letters addressed to Hercule Poirot, a private detective, and not to the police? You *wanted* one of the letters to get lost and reach us too late. But a letter to Scotland Yard could not get lost. So you sent it to a private address. You wanted the police to find out about it only when the murder was safely done.

'Your brother's nightly walk gave you the opportunity. And everyone was thinking about A B C. Nobody thought that you might be guilty.

'After your brother's murder, your purpose was finished. You wanted Mr Cust to be arrested as the murderer, but nobody had noticed him. So you decided that one more murder was necessary. You chose Doncaster as the scene of your next crime. Everything was made very public in the newspapers.

'You gave instructions to Mr Cust to go to Doncaster. In the afternoon he went to a cinema. You were there, too. You stabbed a man and put the *ABC* railway guide under his feet. When Mr Cust left, you followed him and put the bloody knife in his coat pocket.

'And now, my friends, let us imagine how Mr Cust thought about all this. The Andover crime means nothing to him. He is shocked and surprised by the Bexhill crime – he was there at about the same time! Then comes the Churston crime. *Three crimes and he has been at the scene of each of them.* Epilepsy sufferers cannot always remember what they have done ... Then he receives the order to go to Doncaster.

'Doncaster! And the next ABC crime will be in Doncaster. He becomes afraid and tells people he is going to Cheltenham. He goes to Doncaster and visits a cinema in the afternoon. When he gets back to his hotel, he discovers there is blood on his coat.

'So he thinks – *he – he himself is the killer*! He is quite sure of the truth – *he, Alexander Bonaparte Cust*, is a mad killer. He behaves like a hunted animal. He goes back to his rented room in London. He has the knife with him still. He hides it behind the coatstand.

'Then he is warned that the police are coming. *They know!* I don't know why he went to Andover – maybe he wanted to look at the place of the crime, although he could remember nothing about it. He has no money left – he is very tired ... he goes to a police station.

'When I saw him, I knew at once that he was *not* the murderer and that my name *meant* nothing to *him*! I knew that he *thought* he was the murderer!'

'Your idea,' said Franklin Clarke, 'is completely mad!'

'No, Mr Clarke. I found the stick which you used in the Andover and Churston murders in a cupboard at Churston. An ordinary stick with a thick handle. Two people from the cinema in Doncaster recognised your photograph. Milly Higley, the waitress at Bexhill, remembered you. And you left a fingerprint on Cust's typewriter.'

Clarke sat silently for a minute. Then he said, 'You win, Monsieur Poirot!'

He took a small gun out of his pocket and held it to his head. He tried to shoot it, but the gun didn't work. Clarke stared at it in surprise.

'No, Mr Clarke,' said Poirot. 'Perhaps you noticed that I had a new servant today – a friend of mine. He used to be a clever thief. He removed your gun from your pocket and made it safe. Then he put it back. No, Mr Clarke, there will be no easy death for you. Your crime was not at all English – not *fair*.'

Two detectives from Scotland Yard came out from the next room. One of them was Crome. They arrested Franklin Clarke and took him away.

As the door behind Franklin Clarke closed, I am sorry to say that I started to laugh. Poirot looked at me in surprise.

'It's because you told him his crime wasn't fair,' I said.

'It was quite true. It was very cruel – not only the murder of his brother, but to shut a man away for ever in a prison for mad people. Like a living death. *To catch a fox and put him in a box and never let him go!* That is not sport – not *fair*.'

Megan Barnard said, 'I can't believe it – I can't. Is it true?'

'Yes, mademoiselle,' said Poirot. 'It's finished.'

He turned to Fraser.

'Mademoiselle Megan was always afraid that you were responsible for the second crime.'

'I thought so myself at one time,' said Donald Fraser quietly.

'Because of your dream? Your dream has a very natural explanation. In it you find that one sister is being replaced by the other. Mademoiselle Megan is taking the place of her sister in your heart. But you feel guilty so you try to kill the thought. Do not be afraid to forget,' said Poirot gently. 'Mademoiselle Megan is very special. She has a wonderful heart.'

Donald Fraser's eyes lit up.

'I believe you're right,' he said.

We all crowded round Poirot, asking questions.

'Why did you ask us those truth questions, Poirot?'

'I wanted to see Franklin Clarke's face when I asked my question of Mademoiselle Thora. His eyes were full of hate and anger.'

'Franklin Clarke knew it was the end for him when you told him about the fingerprint on the typewriter,' I said.

'Yes, they are useful – fingerprints. I told him that to please you.'

'But, Poirot,' I cried, 'wasn't it true?'

'Not at all, *mon ami*,' said Hercule Poirot.

◆

A few days later we had a visit from Mr Alexander Bonaparte Cust. He shook Poirot's hand and said, 'Do you know, a newspaper has actually offered me a hundred pounds if I tell them about my life. I – I – really don't know what to do about it.'

'You should not accept a hundred,' said Poirot. 'Say that five hundred is your price. And tell the other newspapers about it as well. You must realise that you are a very famous man. Probably the most famous man in England.'

Mr Cust looked very happy.

'Do you know, I believe you're right, Monsieur Poirot,' said Mr Cust. 'The money will be nice – very nice. I'll have a little holiday ... And then I want to give a nice wedding present to Lily Marbury – really a dear girl.'

'You are quite right,' said Poirot. 'And – just a word – what about a visit to an eye doctor? The reason for those headaches is probably that you need new glasses.'

'Do you think so?' Mr Cust shook him warmly by the hand. 'You're a very great man, Monsieur Poirot.'

When Mr Cust had left, my old friend smiled across at me.

'So, Hastings, we went hunting once more, did we not?'

1 Work with two or three other students. You are going to play a game called 'Truth or Lie'.

TRUTH OR LIE?

What do you think of Hercule Poirot, Inspector Crome?

Poirot? I really admire him. He's the best detective in England!

Each of you should choose a different character from the list below. The other students in your group have to ask your character three questions that can be answered from information in the story. You must answer two of the questions truthfully, but lie in your answer to the other one. The other students must guess which answer is a lie.

Megan Barnard	Donald Fraser	Thora Grey	Mary Drower
Alexander Bonaparte Cust		Captain Hastings	Hercule Poirot

2 Work with two other students and have this conversation. You are Tom Hartigan, Lily Marbury and Mrs Marbury. You have read the newspaper reports about the ABC murder in Doncaster. You are talking about Mr Cust and deciding whether you should go to the police.

Tom Hartigan: You think that Mr Cust might be the ABC murderer. You know he was in Bexhill, Churston and Doncaster, and you are worried about Lily. You want to go to the police.

Lily Marbury: You feel sorry for Mr Cust. You have known him for two years. He is rather strange, but you like him. You don't think he can be a murderer.

Mrs Marbury: You are not sure what to do. You like Mr Cust, but you are worried that he could be dangerous. You certainly want him to leave your home.

1 You are Mary Drower. You have been asked by Poirot to act as secretary for the Special Legion and keep a record of the first meeting. Complete the notes.

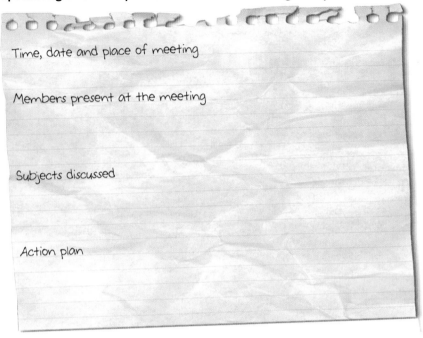

Time, date and place of meeting

Members present at the meeting

Subjects discussed

Action plan

2 Now write a report of the meeting, using the information in your notes.

6 September

Record of the First Meeting of the Special Legion

The meeting took place at M Hercule Poirot's apartment on

Mary Drower (Secretary, Special Legion)

1 Work with two other students. Look at the map of Torquay and the surrounding area and read the information about the town below. Would you go to Torquay on holiday?

The Queen of the English Riviera

In the nineteenth century Torquay, on the south coast of Devon, was called the 'Queen of the Riviera'. Like Rome, it is attractively situated on seven green hills. The area is known as the Riviera because it has a warm climate and is near the sea. You can find Mediterranean plants and flowers growing in the gardens there.

Torquay is the birthplace of Agatha Christie, who wrote *The ABC Murders* and many other detective stories. She was born on 15 September 1890 and spent much of her life in the area. Although Torquay is still in some ways a traditional seaside town, it now feels modern and international. There are many cafés, restaurants and shops, and an exciting night-life.

Torquay is a very popular coastal town for tourists, with beautiful sea views. The historic fishing port is busy with pleasure boats of all sizes as well as fishermen. You can relax by walking on the wide sandy beaches or by swimming in the sea. You can visit interesting places like Kents Cavern, where 450,000-year-old tools have been found underground, and where ghost shows are held on summer nights.

The town can be reached easily by air, road and railway. There are plenty of places to stay, as Torquay has more than 500 hotels as well as guest-houses, holiday flats and areas for camping. It is a wonderful place for a holiday, with something for everyone.

⑬

2 What have you learnt about Torquay? Make notes below.
Add more information from the Internet if you are able to.

Situation	
Famous people	
Reasons to visit	
Places of interest in the area	
Getting there	
Places to stay	

3 In your groups, find information about another popular seaside
holiday town, in Britain or in another country, and make notes below.

Situation	
Famous people	

4 Use your notes to write a page for a tourist brochure for your chosen town. If you have maps and pictures, use a larger piece of paper.

A Perfect Place for a Holiday!

Come to ...., the ....

....

....

....

....

....

....

....

....

....

....

....

....

....

....

....

....

....

....

....

....